Shay stirred n
She'd gone to bed
full hour after that ⸻, ⸻ his time
until he was sure she was in a deep sleep. Only then did
he dare lower himself to rest on top of the comforter.
Waking her now would ruin everything.

Shay rolled to her side, her dark auburn hair sliding
off her bare shoulder. Every muscle in his body tensed,
but she nuzzled into the pillow, and settled back into
slow, rhythmic breaths.

He exhaled and waited for a silent count to one
hundred before easing out of the bed. Cautious of every
step, he left her bedroom and passed through the hall. In
the kitchen, he poured himself a glass of water from the
sink and drank it down in large gulps.

He leaned on the counter and stared at his
reflection in the windowpane. All color had reduced to
black and white thanks to the night beyond, and the
hard angles of his face twisted into a smirk.

After weeks of Shay dominating his thoughts, this
night had finally arrived. Things were in motion. It was
almost more than he could stand.

Cielo

by

Josie Grey

To Betsy & Chip

Cielo

Cover Art by *Diana Carlile*

The Wild Rose Press, Inc.
PO Box 708
Adams Basin, NY 14410-0708
Visit us at www.thewildrosepress.com

Publishing History
First Edition, 2022
Trade Paperback ISBN 978-1-5092-4478-2
Digital ISBN 978-1-5092-4479-9

Published in the United States of America

Dedication

To my critique partners who made this possible.

Acknowledgments

I am eternally grateful for the support my family gave me throughout this process. Especially my husband, for recognizing this was a dream come to life and my mother-in-law, for her unwavering encouragement.

My editor at The Wild Rose Press, Dianne Rich, for your patience as I figured out this process. You are a saint for putting up with my unending emails and never failing to answer the millions of questions I had. I appreciate so much that you really saw my story and helped to make it into its best possible version.

I could have never done this without the help of the many, many critique partners that I've had along the way. Every single of one you that gave me feedback on earlier drafts helped to make this possible, but there were a few of you who devoted more time and energy to my writing than I could have ever imagined. Ellie Fredericks and Nancy Ann Rose, you two taught me how to write (painstakingly and line-by-line at times), all while being so kind and encouraging along the way. I can't thank either of you enough. Sagar Megharaj, your attention to detail and wonderful sense of humor were always exactly what I needed. Michael Swaim, you never failed to get what I was going for, then helped to make it better than I had it in the first place. Thank you all.

Voss Editing, I count my lucky stars that I was somehow able to find you. There's no way to thank you enough for the incredible amount of time and energy you've put into my stories. I absolutely wouldn't have gotten this far without you.

Sharing my work with all of you has truly been an honor. Thank you from the bottom of my heart.

Chapter 1

Portland, Maine

Shay stirred next to him, and he held his breath. She'd gone to bed later than usual. Still, he'd waited a full hour after that before joining her, biding his time until he was sure she was in a deep sleep. Only then did he dare lower himself to rest on top of the comforter. Waking her now would ruin everything.

Shay rolled to her side, her dark auburn hair sliding off her bare shoulder. Every muscle in his body tensed, but she nuzzled into the pillow, and settled back into slow, rhythmic breaths.

He exhaled and waited for a silent count to one hundred before easing out of the bed. Cautious of every step, he left her bedroom and passed through the hall. In the kitchen, he poured himself a glass of water from the sink and drank it down in large gulps.

He leaned on the counter and stared at his reflection in the windowpane. All color had reduced to black and white thanks to the night beyond, and the hard angles of his face twisted into a smirk.

After weeks of Shay dominating his thoughts, this night had finally arrived. Things were in motion. It was almost more than he could stand.

He rinsed and dried the glass, replacing it in the cabinet exactly where he'd found it. With confident strides, he crossed the kitchen and opened the door to a small utility closet. He stepped inside, careful to avoid the floorboard that squeaked. Last time he'd been in her apartment he'd made a point to remember which one it was.

He flipped the electrical box open and reset each breaker. Clicking it shut, he left the closet as carefully as he'd gone in and returned to her bedroom for one last glimpse.

She was perfect. Her face, a calm spot in the storm of his thoughts, was peaceful, relaxed in sleep. He dug his fingernails into his palms to stop himself from smoothing her hair away from where it had fallen across her cheek. He'd played with fire enough for one night.

On her nightstand, the digital display of her alarm clock now blinked 12:01, on and off. Perfect. He'd watched her bedtime routine through the window plenty of times over the past three weeks. Every night, she'd set the alarm clock instead of relying on her phone to wake her, but this wasn't the night to take chances. He turned around and powered off her cell phone where it was charging on the dresser.

His heart galloped as he backed out of her room and crept to the bathroom. Slipping out the same window he'd come in through, he left it cracked open and popped the screen back in. He kept to the shadows until reaching the sidewalk where he quickened his pace.

The waiting had been excruciating, but in just a few hours it would be over. He'd finally get the chance to properly introduce himself. He reached his car down the block, turned his key in the ignition, and the Lexus' engine purred to life. A smile spread across his face as he eased the car onto the street.

Shay had no clue her life was about to change.

Chapter 2

Shay

Flustered and late, Shay tried to slip out of the employee changing room unnoticed. The chance of that happening dissipated when the sharp click of her manager's shoes on the tile floor preceded him around the corner.

"You're killing me, Shay." He shook his head but didn't look up from his clipboard or slow as he passed.

"Sorry, Raul," she called to his back and tied her apron as a smile tugged at the corners of her mouth.

If she were in trouble, he would've stopped. At least her alarm clock had picked a good day to not go off. Sunday morning was the easiest shift of the week at St. George's with the most overpriced and pretentious a la carte menu in all of Portland, Maine, turning into the most overpriced and pretentious buffet brunch. It was way less work for the waitstaff than a regular shift, and even though the doors opened at nine, the rush wouldn't begin until ten or eleven. It would've been pushing her luck if she'd stopped at her usual coffee spot, but she'd sacrificed that on the off-chance Raul was in a bad mood.

She pushed through the swinging door to enter the kitchen and was greeted with a bustle of activity. Line cooks filled trays with Eggs Benedict, Belgian waffles, bread pudding, roasted potatoes, and freshly made pastries for the waitstaff to ferry to the dining room.

Shay grabbed two kitchen towels to shield her hands and picked up the next piping hot tray in line to go. As she lifted it, she glanced up and met the crystal blue eyes of the sous chef, Roman Garcia, across the line.

His eyebrows rose. "I thought you weren't coming in, *mi cielo*. My heart was starting to break." His slight Colombian accent thickened as he spoke.

"Well, pick up the pieces, Roman. And get back to work before George sees you wasting time hitting on the waitresses." Despite her serious tone, Shay wasn't quite able to suppress her enjoyment at his shameless flirting.

"Not waitresses, just one waitress. And it won't be a waste when you finally agree to be Mrs. Garcia." He grinned, unapologetic.

The voice of the restaurant's owner and head chef, George, boomed from the other end of the line. "Roman, get the basil."

"Coming now." He backed away but didn't break eye contact with Shay until she turned and shook her head. She'd worked in enough restaurants over the past six years to know that playful banter was part of the culture. Still, Roman got to her in a way that no one else did.

A few trips later, the buffet was set up, and Shay snuck away to pour a cup of coffee for herself behind the service station. Her favorite bartender, Alex, reached around her, grabbing napkins from the overhead cabinet to restock the bar.

He eyed the mug in her hand. "No mocha-capa-whatever for you today?"

Despite only knowing Alex for the six weeks since he'd started at George's, he'd become her closest friend.

"No. The power went out during the night. My alarm clock reset, so it didn't go off this morning."

"Alarm clock? Girl, you're living in the nineties. Just use your phone."

"But the clock I use wakes me up to the sound of birds. It's really nice." She laughed as he rolled his eyes. It was stupid, but it was one of the few things that had stayed consistent in her life. Those birds had woken her up back when her parents were alive, through three years in a foster home, and through her entire undergraduate degree in psychology.

"Well, good thing you made it. Roman was about ready to send out a search party. He's already asked me twice where you were."

"He would've found someone else to flirt with if I'd given it another ten minutes." She dismissed the comment but couldn't ignore the flash of warmth it ignited in her. Better to not go down that path and end up a notch on his bedpost.

Roman's reputation as a serial dater was something Shay had found out about practically two seconds into her first shift six months ago. The waitress training her went over all the important things. "You get one employee meal per shift. Polish one rack of silverware before you leave for the night. And watch out, Roman hits on anything with boobs."

The warning came right before her trainer led Shay into the kitchen for the first time. As quick introductions were called across the line, Shay picked out Roman immediately. He'd leaned against the long metal table that separated the cooking line from the waitstaff and food runners.

Her trainer smirked in Roman's direction. "And finally, last but not least, our sous chef, Roman."

Resting his arms on the top shelf, he'd peered under the heat lamp that had yet to be turned on for the night. When his deep blue eyes met Shay's, her breath caught at the intensity.

One side of his mouth tugged into a grin. "*Mi cielo.*" He paused, and the shadow of a smile faded into a serious expression that sent a jolt to her toes when he spoke again. "What are you doing for the rest of your life?"

It wasn't the kind of line that would've usually gotten to her. But when she opened her mouth to say something sharp back, she found herself with no reply. He wasn't even close to her type. His well-built stature wasn't short, but he didn't break six feet. And the combination of his close-cropped light-brown hair and blue eyes made him a far cry from the tall, dark, and rugged look that Shay usually favored. Despite that, there was an immediate and annoying attraction that only seemed to grow with each shift they worked together.

Alex, the bartender, pulled her out of her thoughts. "You feel like getting tipsy tonight? There's a new spot on South Street serving drinks in buckets. It's like they looked into my soul and found what was missing."

Shay sighed. "I wish. Tonight's my volunteer night on the crisis line."

"Uh, yikes. Suicide watch. That's less fun."

She snapped a towel at him. "Don't even joke

about that. I'll call you when I'm done. If you're not too many buckets in, maybe I'll meet you."

"I'll pace myself." Alex took his napkins and left Shay to finish her coffee. Every minute or so, she peeked around the wall that hid the service station from the dining room to make sure her section was still empty.

It was doubtful she'd be up for a bucket of booze by the end of her day. The one use her psychology degree got was her weekly shift at her alma mater's student's crisis line. Every fourth-year psych major had to do ten shifts there, and it had been one of her favorite parts of the program. She liked it enough that she'd continued after graduating six months ago. Tonight would be dominated by answering the line dedicated for students to call when they were feeling overwhelmed. Even though it was fulfilling, it could be draining.

Shay peered into the dining room and saw there was a four-top waiting for her. She took a last sip of her coffee and placed the mug in a bus bucket. No point in saving it. Once things got going on the restaurant floor, she'd forget it existed.

Pasting a smile on her face, she walked across the dining room. Out of the corner of her eye, she saw Roman pass a bucket of ice across the bar to Alex, and the butterflies that seemed to always be waiting for him stirred to life in her stomach.

She hated how much she wanted to take him up on one of his hundreds of offers to go out. But she needed this job. Starting a relationship with a rising star chef who had a reputation of going through women at a record pace would be one of the fastest ways to lose it.

It was easy to understand why so many women

were drawn to him. He somehow managed to walk the line between cocky asshole and the guy who'd save a kitten in a rainstorm. Plus, he had a chiseled bone structure that would look severe, except he constantly smiled like he had an inside joke.

She shook Roman from her mind and pulled her gaze from him to the table of four in front of her. "Good morning. You're welcome to start on the buffet whenever you'd like." She gestured to the spread that took up the entire back wall of the restaurant. "Can I offer you something to drink?"

She took their coffee order and repeated the same process with her next table.

Midmorning, Shay stood at the bar waiting for a drink order to come up when Alex placed two mimosas on her tray and raised his eyebrows at her. "Wow, do you have an admirer."

"Oh, yeah? Who?" Shay glanced around the room while Alex mixed a Bloody Mary. "I'm only interested if he's incredibly handsome and filthy rich."

"I think you're in luck then. Mr. Handsome-Mc-Trust-Fund at table twelve has not taken his eyes off you."

Shay peeked over her shoulder, as Alex discreetly slipped his phone from his apron. The family at table twelve could have just stepped off a yacht in the Hamptons. The son looked to be in his mid-to-late twenties, and Alex was correct. He was classically handsome with a strong jaw, thick blond hair, and light-brown eyes that deepened with a smile when he caught Shay's glance.

Shay turned quickly back to Alex. "He's too pretty to be straight. Maybe he's admiring you, not me."

"I wish, but no. He's straight and single if the internet's correct," Alex said, slipping his phone back into his apron and placing the Bloody Mary next to the mimosas to complete her order.

"How do you know who he is? Is he famous?" She glanced sideways and caught him looking at her again.

"Not him, but his dad is." Alex nodded toward the man at the head of the table. "Jack Matthews. As in millionaire senator, Jack Matthews. I just ran his black card and searched the name."

The group stood to leave but instead of passing by with the rest of his family toward the door, the handsome admirer walked directly toward her.

Alex picked up the full tray. "I'm gonna run these for you, while you get swept off your feet." He left her alone, and she fought the irrational urge to run.

Before she had a chance to escape, the mystery man stopped in front of her with his impossibly white smile. "Hi, Shay."

"Hi." She frowned and cocked her head to the side trying to place him. "I'm sorry, but have we met?"

"Shay, mocha latte, almond milk." He relayed her coffee order.

She exhaled, her frown melting in relief. "You go to GG's."

"Almost every morning. I think I have all the regulars' orders memorized that come in around seven a.m. I'm Kyle, café macchiato."

He was vaguely familiar. "I haven't seen you there, but I'm not the most observant until after I've been caffeinated."

"Hey, I get it. I'm not the kind of guy who stands out in a crowd." His glaringly bright smile flashed with the lie. "So, I think it's interesting that today's the first time I don't see you there in weeks, but somehow, I end up being dragged to a brunch where you happen to work. I figured it's a sign I should ask you out. You know, since fate's obviously throwing us together."

It was the first time in months Shay had missed her coffee run, thanks to the power outage. Running into him was a coincidence, but that didn't change her answer. "I'm sorry, right now I don't have time for dating. But I'm flattered by the offer." It was annoyingly accurate. A friend had dragged her to an intro to jewelry making class sophomore year, and it spiraled into an obsession for Shay. The few local shops who carried her items had finally started to sell enough to cover the cost of materials and the space she rented at a local workshop. She believed in her talent enough that she'd put off the thought of grad school to see if she could make a living from her hobby. For now, if she wasn't in her workshop, she was here at George's.

Kyle's smile faded, and Shay reconsidered her knee-jerk reaction. He was handsome and obviously interested in her, plus it would be a good distraction from Roman. She almost changed her mind.

Almost. Until a flicker of anger flared in his eyes. "Are you seriously saying no?"

"It's not that I don't appreciate the offer, but I don't even have time for friends, let alone dating." She doubled down without another thought.

The anger vanished, and his smile returned. "I understand. Well, we'll always have GG's. Maybe you'll notice me now?"

"I'm sure I will," she said.

He tapped a fist on the bar and bit his lip, giving

her one last once over. "I'll be seeing you, Shay."

She exhaled a sigh of relief when he finally turned to go, then wound her way through the dining room, pushing through the swinging double doors into the kitchen.

"Did you just turn that man down?" Alex followed close behind. "You do not say 'no' when someone who looks like that asks you out."

"Apparently I do." Shay shrugged.

Roman came over and leaned against a refrigerator. "Of course, she'd say 'no' if some other man tried to make a pass. She's hopelessly in love with me."

"You wish." Shay shook her head at him.

"You know I do." His eyes glowed when they caught hers.

"Shay, you just turned down a millionaire by insinuating you're a loser, if I heard correctly," Alex said. "I can't even live the high life vicariously. I'm gonna go start day drinking." He flung open the door and strode back into the dining room.

Roman pushed himself off the fridge. "It's good to know you won't be after me for my money when I finally wear you down."

Shay didn't look at him as she pulled a clean rack of champagne flutes off the drying line to bring back to the bar with her. "You'll eventually stop."

"Sure I will. When you agree to marry me. Until then, what can I make you for lunch, *mi cielo*?" His deep voice rumbled, pleasantly raising the little hairs at the base of her neck.

****

The rest of her shift passed by quickly. Shay tugged off her apron after the buffet had been broken

12

down and the staff for the dinner shift had trickled in. A few steps behind Alex, she entered the changing room, pocketing her cash after tipping out the busboys. Roman sat on one of the benches, his hand being bandaged by their pastry chef, Janet, who continued to work despite being old enough to retire.

"This will hold you 'til you get to the hospital, but you're going to need stitches. If that knife slipped another centimeter, you'd be searching for your fingertip right now." She secured the last of the tape.

Shay walked over and examined his bandaged hand with concern. "Are you okay?"

"I don't know. I may need a nurse. Are you busy tonight?" He cocked an eyebrow.

Janet rolled her eyes. "He's fine." She turned to Roman. "Can you drive yourself?"

"I'll call a cab." He stood, slipping off his chef coat, careful of his injury. The T-shirt beneath left his well-muscled arms exposed and momentarily weakened Shay's resolve. Until he spoke again, and her heart dropped.

"Gisella's still here. She took my car to go deal with some details at the property she bought up north." He reached into his locker and took his wallet off the top shelf, tucking it into his back pocket with his good hand.

"Smart girl. Making that modeling money work for her." Janet finished packing up the first aid box and snapped the lid closed.

"Yeah, I wish she'd spend some on a car, so I don't have to keep giving up mine when she's in town." He looked at Shay. "I'll text you my room number if they admit me, so you can send flowers."

He winked and left, seemingly unaware that he'd taken all the air from the room with one word. *Gisella.*

Shay stared at the door as it swung closed behind him.

She'd only learned of Gisella Medija's existence last week when she overheard one of the busboys giving him a hard time while she was getting bread for a table. Even with her limited Spanish, the gestures he made left no doubt what he was insinuating he'd like to do with Gisella. Roman dropped the ladle in his hand and stalked, red-faced, toward the now-running busboy. A string of curses followed the kid as he disappeared out the kitchen door laughing, almost knocking over an entering waitress on his way. Roman had huffed out a breath and shook his head returning to the line.

"Watch it, Corey," the waitress, Rachel, called out the door, steading her tray. Her gaze followed Roman as she came up next to Shay. "What was that about?"

"Corey was saying lewd things about a *Gisella*, and Roman lost it."

"Yeah, that never goes over well. These guys can't help themselves. Gisella's a demi-god." She picked up a breadbasket and tossed a roll in. "She's gorgeous," another roll, "famous," roll, "rich..." Reaching past Shay, Rachel grabbed a carefully sculpted dish of butter from the cooler and added it to her basket. "Which is why the guys give him such a hard time when she breezes into town and into his apartment."

Shay's heart dropped. "She lives with him?" If anyone knew about Roman's personal life, it'd be Rachel. She'd worked at George's for years.

Rachel scrunched her lips. "I wouldn't say she lives with him. It's more she stays there when she has breaks from work. Sometimes a few days, sometimes a few weeks, then she's off, visiting places I can only dream about."

"What does she do?" Shay regretted the question before it fully left her lips. She didn't need to know any of this.

Rachel backed up toward the door then pushed through. "She's a supermodel."

"Of course she is," Shay mumbled, shoveling bread into her own basket, haphazardly.

Later that night, unable to resist her morbid curiosity, Shay had looked her up, immediately wishing she hadn't. After seeing pictures of her, Shay could understand why Roman at twenty-eight, wasn't deterred by the fact that Gisella was nine years older. She was the kind of gorgeous where age didn't matter. Tall, thin but curvy, long wavy black hair, doe eyes, and lips that seemed impossibly full. It wouldn't be a competition with Gisella for Roman's attention. It would be a slaughter.

Over the past few months, there'd been a noticeable decrease in the number of women Roman usually paraded through the restaurant. Shay had been naïve enough to think maybe she'd been the reason, but this made more sense. His on and off girlfriend bought property here, probably making them more on than off.

Let her go play nurse. Shay slammed her locker closed and slung her bag over her shoulder.

"Uh-oh." Alex raised his eyebrows. "The G-word?"

"Shut up." Shay pushed past him, only to have him follow.

"Come on. Don't be like that. No one can blame

you for catching some feelings. Roman is a smooth talker, and he lays it on thick with you. If I didn't know better, I'd think there was something really there for him from the way he looks at you." They stepped out the front door and walked to the nearby alley, where the employees parked.

"Yeah, well, you do know better. And so do I. I'm so stupid. I wouldn't have a chance against Gisella. Jesus, I don't even know why I'm talking about it. He flirts with me like he flirts with everyone. That's it."

"You know I would normally jump into your pity party with both feet and tell you what an idiot you are for falling for him…" Alex paused.

"But?"

"But…I think you have a reason for falling for him."

"Come on, Alex. You're supposed to talk me out of it."

"I'm sorry. But I thought he was into you, too, until this Gisella business started."

"That doesn't help me feel any better. It just shows you're an idiot, too." Shay gave him a half-smile through her misery.

"Okay, well, remember a couple of weeks ago when you moved, and the moving company canceled last minute? Who showed up with his friends and their trucks? Roman." Alex looked smugly at her. "And how about the fact he always takes his staff meals at the same time as you? Or what he did for your birthday?"

Shay couldn't help but smile when she thought about her birthday last month. Roman had gone out of his way to make it special, plus Gisella's name never came up. It had been great.

Alex brought her out of the pleasant memory, back to the irritating present. "It went way past flirting for him, if you ask me."

"Yeah, well, it doesn't matter now." She hugged him as they approached her car. "Thanks for not letting me be an idiot alone."

"Aw, sweetie, anytime." He kissed the top of her head and backed away toward his own car.

****

Shay found a spot near the student center and made it to the Crisis Line office as her shift was starting. She waved hello to the supervisor for the evening, a professor she recognized from when she took Intro to Psychology, a long four years ago. There was always a specially trained professional on hand in case someone suicidal called in. Luckily, that was rare. Most calls were students venting about their course load, sad about a breakup, or people who were simply lonely and wanted to talk. Other nights, no one called at all.

Shay took a seat in an unoccupied cubicle and pulled out a sketch pad to occupy her time until she received a call. It was over an hour before the phones rang in unison. The girl seated to her right was first in line for the call.

"Hello, this is operator 675. How are you tonight?" There was a pause as she listened. "Sure. Hold on one sec." Sarah called out, "There's a Toby on the phone requesting operator 1125."

"That's me. I got it. Thanks." Shay had been expecting the call and picked up the line. "Hi, Toby."

"Well, good evening, Miss 1125. How are you on this beautiful summer night?" A familiar southern drawl came through the line.

"I'm good. How are you doing?" Shay had dubbed Toby her "frequent flyer," since he called every shift she worked. They weren't allowed to give out their names, to protect their privacy, but each operator had a specific ID assigned to them, and he'd requested her each Sunday night since his first call two months ago.

"I can't really complain. Busy, but I'm managing." From the previous calls Shay had received from Toby, she'd learned he was an IT and computer engineering double major who sometimes became overwhelmed with the demands of his course load.

"Good. Hopefully, you're finding some time to relax." Shay twirled the phone cord around one finger and glanced at the clock—two hours left.

"A bit, here and there. I'll tell you, I'm missing the Texas ranch life right about now. A thing I never thought I'd say. How about you? You get homesick?"

"Not terribly, but it's normal if you are. Maine must have been a bit of a culture shock." Shay carefully sidestepped giving out any personal details and shifted the conversation back to Toby. "Any plans for a visit home?"

"Nah, nothing soon. Maybe for the holidays, especially if my folks aren't going to be around."

"You miss the place more than the people?"

"You could say that the feeling's probably mutual. Once the picture for the holiday card is taken, we're not usually all in the same room willingly again until we need to make appearances at Christmas parties."

"That must be a little lonely," Shay said. Toby had touched on his feeling of isolation within his family a few times before.

"I guess. I never really thought about it."

"If you feel like that about your family, sometimes relationships with friends can be a helpful thing to foster."

There was a long pause before he answered. "How about you, 1125? You sound a little down today. How's your day going?"

Shay recognized that maybe she'd touched a nerve. Toby had never once mentioned a friend. She lightened the conversation. "My day's been good. Busy as usual. I like to think I'm getting better at handling the chaos." She hoped he picked up on her subtle implication that he was not alone. Trying to strike a balance with new obligations was something everyone went through, and it would get better.

"Well, I hope you make some time for fun in your busy schedule. I gotta run. Talk to you next Sunday?"

"Talk to you then, Toby. If you have any comments or concerns about this call there's a link to click on the school's homepage, and as you already know my operator number is 1125." She delivered the line they were supposed to end all calls with.

"I'll give you a glowing review. Goodnight, 1125."

"Take care." Shay hung up, glad that Toby sounded lighter than the first time she talked to him. During his initial call, Shay had worried he was suicidal. She'd had the supervisor listen in, but Shay was able to navigate the conversation into safer territory, and they never had to intervene. It was one of her success stories and a big reason why she'd agreed to continue after graduation when the program supervisor had offered it. If her jewelry business didn't work out, she had the psychology degree to fall back on and even if she didn't love it, at least she was good at it.

Shay replaced the phone in its cradle and picked up her sketch pad to trace out a design for a bracelet that she'd been seeing in her mind all day. Her attention returned to avoiding all thoughts Roman related.

Chapter 3

Roman

It was after nine p.m. when Roman finally arrived home from the ER. He used his unbandaged hand to open the apartment door and was greeted by a squealing Gisella.

"It's done." She flung herself into his arms and squeezed.

"Careful," he cautioned, raising his hand overhead to avoid further injury from her enthusiasm. "That's great, Gisella."

She caught sight of the bandage, and her smile faded as she pulled away from him. "Oh, *mi amor*, what happened?"

"Nothing. Just a few stitches. I'll be back at work tomorrow. Come on." He gestured for her to follow him into the kitchen. "I want to hear all about it, but I'm starving." He started pulling meat and cheese from the fridge to make a sandwich.

Gisella came up behind him and nudged him out of the way. "Here. Let me do that. I can handle making a sandwich."

"I don't know…I'm pretty sure I've seen you burn water." He laughed as she shoved him.

"Ha-ha. Keep it up, and I'll cut your other hand, *pendejo*." She added a few slices of bread to the stack of cold cuts and brought it to the counter.

"So, tell me, Miss Real Estate Mogul, is it as good as you hoped?" Roman sank into one of the chairs at the kitchen table and stretched a kink out of his neck.

Gisella's eyes sparkled as she put a sandwich on a plate and placed it in front of him. "It is." She took a seat at the head of the table and clasped her hands together. "Oh, Roman. Wait until you see it. The renovations have made the property as beautiful as it used to be. I would've paid twice as much."

"That's great. So, you're on track to open on time then?" Roman took a huge bite of the sandwich.

"Next week. All the staff's trained...except I've left the position of head chef open. And there are a couple of houses by the lake." She paused and raised her eyebrows. "Ever dream of living lakeside?"

Roman sighed. "Gisella, I haven't given it that much thought yet. It would be a huge step. I don't know if I'm ready."

"You've designed the menus, and they're your recipes. Why don't you want to fully commit?"

Shay. Roman shook his head. It was insane to base life-altering decisions on a woman who turned him down on a daily basis. Boy, was he his father's son.

Gisella broke the silence. "Come look at it. See if that helps you make the decision. When's your next day off?"

"Saturday."

"Perfect. It's only a two-hour drive, but we'll stay over so we don't have to rush." Gisella's phone pinged on the table next to her. She read the message then glanced at Roman's hand. "My ride's downstairs. You need anything before I go?"

"No, I'm good. Is Pete going with you?"

"It's just dinner with friends. I won't even be that late." She ducked out of the room, returning a minute later with a pair of heels in her hand that she slid on.

"And is Pete going?" Roman asked again.

"No." She glared at him and added, "I'll be with a whole group of people. It'll be okay. Plus, I don't need a bodyguard for every single thing I do."

"No, but he's new. It's smart for you to see if you two are a good fit in low-key settings before he works a high-profile event with you."

"We clicked right away. Stop worrying. He's good. I'm good."

"Just be careful." Roman took his empty plate to the sink. "If you go out after dinner, call Pete. Friends or no friends, don't take chances."

"I will. Love you. See you in the morning." She kissed his cheek as she blew by, grabbing her purse off the counter.

Roman flicked off the lights and walked to his room to collapse on the bed.

****

Monday had dragged, as it always did, since it was Shay's day off. Tuesday afternoon Roman walked into the employee changing room whistling and broke into a huge smile at the sight of her tugging on the crisp white button-up shirt that was part of the waitstaff's uniform.

"Welcome back. How was your day of freedom yesterday, *mi cielo*?"

"Hi, Roman." She glanced over her shoulder at him with a quick smile. "I wouldn't call a four-hour webinar on how to run a small business followed by doing a week's worth of laundry freedom, but I got in a few hours at the workshop, and it was nice to not be on my feet for ten hours."

"Drive and beauty. No one can blame me for falling in love." A familiar excitement stirred in his chest when she turned toward him. Before he met Shay, he didn't think the saying "she took my breath away" was something that actually happened to people.

Shay smiled up at him as she passed by. "Laying it on thick today, I see. Careful, or the other waitresses will get jealous." She pushed through the door before he could think of something to keep the exchange going.

He grabbed a clean chef jacket off the rack and pulled it on as he left the room.

The kitchen was in the lull between lunch and dinner, and Roman started a prep list as soon as he entered. He gathered the line cooks, went over the specials, and doled out the prep work assignments. He assigned himself to work on the cioppino that would hopefully be the highlight of that evening's menu.

As the dinner rush began, Roman fell into the rhythm of the kitchen. It was what he loved—being busy, creating, giving people food that made them happy to pay the exorbitant prices George continued to raise. The kitchen operated like a loud, wild ballet. On Shay's first night working, she'd slipped in seamlessly to the chaotic dance and caught Roman's attention. Then his world had stopped when her eyes met his. Golden-brown, kind, and sharp. He was done for.

The fact that she refused his initial attempts at asking her out drove him crazy at first. Then he was grateful. He needed to get his shit together before he started something with her. He was ready to move on from George's but hadn't landed on a plan yet. Now there was Gisella complicating things. He took a deep breath, not wanting to rush that decision. For now, he'd avoid thinking about it.

He looked across the room to where two waitresses shared a quick kiss at the soup station and whistled through his teeth. "Come on...Sarah...Melody. Please, this is a workplace. Plus, you'll make the rest of us jealous, flaunting your love." He shook his head in mock disappointment.

Both women turned to him wearing matching dubious expressions. The shorter of the two, Sarah, said, "I doubt you have a reason to be jealous, Roman. You get more ass than a toilet seat."

The line cooks in earshot laughed, and Roman followed up with, "Don't mistake quantity for quality."

"Come on. You wouldn't even know if you were missing out on quality at the rate you go," Melody chimed in.

A hitch of irritation coursed through Roman. He'd dated a lot of women. It wasn't a secret. What pissed him off was when people got the impression that he was callous about it. He was upfront about not looking for anything serious with all the women he took out. He respected every single one, and a fair share didn't even progress beyond a good night kiss.

Shay pushed through the door and went to the cooler where they kept the side salads.

"See, there's quality right now. I know it when I see it." Roman kept up the light façade despite his momentary irritation.

"Do I even want to know?" Shay asked the other servers as she stacked plates on her arm to carry out.

Melody shook her head and held the door open for Shay to return to the dining room. "No. Definitely not."

Soon after, they got slammed with a rush that lasted up until Shay got let go for the night.

"You hungry, *mi cielo*?" Roman called when Shay picked up the desserts for her last table of the night.

"Yes, but I think I'm too tired to eat." Her long auburn hair had started to escape her ponytail, and it trailed in wisps around her face as she moved.

"Too tired for herb-poached salmon?"

"It's 86ed." With both hands full with dessert plates, she nodded toward the whiteboard next to the door that kept a running list of items the kitchen had run out of.

"I saved us a piece." He grinned and a smile spread across her face. She loved salmon.

"You're going to get yourself in trouble," Shay scolded.

"I'm already in trouble." *Truer words were never spoken.* "Meet me on the loading dock in fifteen."

She rolled her eyes but nodded.

Twenty minutes later, she took a seat on the overturned five-gallon bucket he'd set up across from his own. Between them, a plate that could have been an exhibit in an art show sat on a stack of boxes.

"Ooohhh. Is that the lemon risotto?" Her eyes widened.

"It is. Dig in." He passed a fork across to her and waited to take a bite of his own so he could watch her reaction.

When she put the first bite in her mouth, her eyes closed, and she moaned. "Oh my God. That is so good."

He smiled and took a bite himself. It was good. It

would've been better if George had let him add the sauce he made, but if Shay was happy, he was happy.

"Try this." He dipped the tip of a spoon into a small ramekin containing the rejected sauce and held it out to her.

She tased it and licked her lips. "That's even better. Let me guess."

He waited, and she dipped the spoon again.

"Lemon, garlic, dill, and something sweet?"

He nodded. He loved it when she tried to guess his recipes.

"Honey?"

"Just a touch. You're getting better." He took the spoon back and tasted it himself. "So, how were tips?" *Dill. It needed more dill.*

"Really good." She nodded as she ate. "I would make a crack about overpriced food bringing in overpriced tips, but this is worth the price tag. Are you done for the night?"

"Nah, I'm closing."

"You should get back up there before they notice you snuck away."

"The worst they can do is fire me, and that may be doing me a favor at this point."

"Why? Looking for a new pool of waitresses to flirt with?" She scraped up the last of the risotto.

"There's no one I'd rather flirt with than you." He couldn't help himself when she set him up like that. The truth about his feelings was always simmering below the surface whenever she was around.

"Oh? And what would Gisella say about that?" Shay raised her eyebrows.

A single laugh escaped him. "There's no way I'd

willingly discuss you with Gisella." It wasn't technically true. He'd mentioned Shay more than once to Gisella. Her name came up way less in conversation than it did in his mind, but it was hard to edit Shay out of enough work stories to not make Gisella suspicious.

The door burst open, and two busboys came out, hauling full bags of trash on their way to the dumpster across the parking lot.

"Busted." Shay bent down to pick up her purse. "Thanks for dinner. I'll see you tomorrow." She jumped off the loading dock.

He called after her, "Hey, I almost forgot." He reached down and picked up a to-go bag that had been resting near his foot. "For your friend."

Shay took the bag, opened it, and smiled. "T-bone?"

"Only the best for that monster." Roman smirked. He'd helped her move into her new apartment a few weeks ago, and they'd both met her neighbor's giant pit bull. The dog had immediately warmed to Shay, and Roman imagined that affection had only grown since she started sneaking table scraps home shortly after the move.

"Thanks. He'll love it." She gave him one last smile and crossed the back lot to the alley.

Roman watched as she walked away.

He loved these little moments he stole with her. He'd first come up with the idea of using the loading dock for some privacy last month for her birthday. She would have never agreed to let him take her out to celebrate since she turned him down every other time he'd asked, but she hadn't said no to the simplicity of a cupcake followed by cold beers.

It went beyond what he'd hoped for when she'd stayed and chatted with him deep into the night. Looking across the lot now, he watched as she rounded the corner into the alley. A moment later, headlights lit up the night and her little white sedan sped by.

One of the busboys taunted on his way back from the dumpster, "Awww. cheer up. It might not be you. Maybe she has plans with a guy with a nicer loading dock."

"Keep it up, I'll have you gutting fish all day tomorrow." Roman pulled his phone out of his pocket to check the time.

Instead, he found a text from Gisella waiting.

—*Do you still have a tux that fits?*—

—*Yes. Why?*—

Gisella quickly replied.

—*I need you to come with me to a charity thing tomorrow*—

—*I can't. I'm working*—

—*Pretty please…it would mean the world to me*—

Roman thought a moment and replied:

—*Fine. I'll get someone to cover so I can leave early. What time?*—

—*I can pick you up at nine. Thank you! I love you!!!!*—

He could practically hear her excitement through the text. He sighed and tapped out his reply.

—*I love you, too.*—

Chapter 4

Shay

The next morning, Shay stepped into GG's at her regular time and glanced around. Now that she knew to look for him, Kyle was easy to pick out. He sat at the same corner table he'd given her a friendly wave from yesterday. Today, it seemed he was too engrossed in whatever he was doing on his laptop to look up. She glanced over a couple more times as she waited for her order. Her coffee came up, and she had a momentary impulse to go over and say hi. Ignoring it, she walked out into the warm morning air and drove to the local library with her windows down.

A long day at the workshop had seen the completion of her first custom order, a set of hammered silver wrist cuff bracelets. They had come out beautifully, but the work left her shoulders aching for a hot shower. She pushed the want away and walked in for the dinner shift at St. George's. The night ramped up quickly, and she kept reminding herself the crazier it got, the more money went in her pocket. Busy nights were what padded her bank account and would make sure she didn't end up a literal starving artist while her business gained momentum.

She was tapping a pen on her empty tray, waiting for her drink order when a group at the end of the bar caught her eye. They were taking shots, and she picked out a familiar million-dollar smile. Kyle placed his empty glass on the bar and picked up a beer bottle. He met her gaze and slid off his barstool to approach her.

"Night on the town?" she asked.

"No, just a quick drink, then we're grabbing dinner down the street. If you're done soon, you're welcome to join us."

"Thanks, but I'm on till the bitter end tonight."

"Tell them you're coming down with something."

"Unless I leave in an ambulance, my manager wouldn't buy it."

"Do it anyway. What's the worst that can happen?"

"Umm, I get fired, can't pay rent, and end up homeless." Shay set cocktail napkins on her tray.

"I'll pay your rent." There wasn't even a hint of humor.

"Drink's up." Alex placed several full glasses on Shay's tray and rushed back to the next of the order tickets that were flying out of the printer.

She balanced the tray, shaking her head at Kyle's offer. "Have fun." People who had the world at their feet would never understand.

He shrugged. "Had to try." Then turned back to his friends.

The oddness of the encounter stayed with her, and she put her next order in wrong.

"Shit," she mumbled, one second after she hit the button that sent it to the kitchen. She rushed back and stepped into what would look like chaos to the untrained eye but was in fact the choreography of a well-oiled machine of chefs, busboys, wait staff, and food runners, each playing their part. Cutting a straight path to the expediter who directed the whole wild ensemble, she interrupted him.

"Sorry, Chef. That ticket I just sent needs the appetizers to come first. I accidentally sent the whole thing at once."

The expediter nodded. Without looking at her, he pulled a marker out of his breast pocket and drew a line on the ticket separating the apps from the entrees while yelling, "Fire one calamari, one tartar."

"Thanks, Chef." She sighed, relieved he didn't chew her out.

On her way back to the dining room, she searched the line for Roman. She recognized his broad shoulders on the fish station, flipping mussels in a sauté pan over an open flame with one hand and reaching above him for a bowl to plate them with the other. In one motion he slid them from the pan into the bowl and met Shay's eyes as he turned to put them under the heat lamp. His face went from a serious mask of concentration to a grin, and he winked at her before she ducked through the door.

Butterflies. *Fuck.*

As things slowed, the first wave of servers were let go for the night. Shay went back to the kitchen for her employee meal. While still busy, the mode had switched from surviving the rush to maintaining it. Soon it would be a balancing act of closing up as much as possible, while still being functional enough to operate for the trickle of late-night customers.

Before she could give her order to a line cook, Roman called to her, "I made you something special." He walked past carrying a bus bin of pans to be washed and nodded toward the shelf behind her.

She rubbed her hands together as her gaze landed on the tray of perfectly fried, garlic-salted chips. "Oh, I needed this tonight."

St. George's rarely served chips. When they did occasionally pop up as a side to a lunch special, Shay made it a habit to dip them into the mushroom bisque that had become a staple on the menu since Roman first created it. The flavors together were more decadent than should be possible for a bowl of soup.

"I didn't see chips on the special menu tonight." She ladled out a bowl of the silky bisque as he came around the line.

"They weren't," he whispered near her ear as he walked by, sending a cascade of goosebumps from the base of her neck down her arms. He headed in the direction of the locker room unbuttoning his chef coat and called back, *"Buenas noches, mi cielo."*

She ate standing up at a prep table, her heart racing. Somewhere in his busy night, Roman had made time to slice potatoes and fry them. That act risked his life if Chef George caught him making something off menu for a staff member.

She finished, savoring every bite, and went back to the dining room to take over so the other servers could leave. Roman stepped out of the locker room as she passed, and her breath faltered. She'd never seen him in a suit before. Usually, he wore jeans or gym clothes when he left.

"Wow, fancy." She cleared her throat, trying to recover. "Hot date?"

"I'm pretty sure I'm being used for my good looks and charming personality. Charity work on my part, really."

They walked into the dining room to find a stunning brunette in a floor-length, skintight, red dress that showed off her impossibly flawless body. Next to Shay, Roman mumbled something inaudible, then took a deep breath.

The beautiful woman leaned toward him and kissed the air next to his cheek, keeping her perfectly applied lipstick intact.

"Gisella." He pulled back from her. "This is Shay."

Gisella's face lit up, and she smiled warmly. "Shay, it's so nice to meet you." Her speech had the same lyrical inflections as Roman's, but much more pronounced.

Shay pulled her gaze from Gisella's beautifully manicured hand, casually resting on Roman's arm like it belonged there. "Nice to meet you, too. Have a good night."

Shay rushed away to make herself busy. Until that moment, she hadn't realized a part of her had let things with Roman get too carried away in her head. Seeing Gisella through a computer screen was one thing, but in person provided the concrete evidence of exactly how far out of her league Roman was. Hot tears burned behind her eyes from embarrassment for thinking his playful flirting even had the possibility of being more.

Raul came up next to Shay. "Was that Gisella?"

"Um, yeah." She fought to cover up the emotion in her voice.

"Wow, she gets more beautiful every time I see her."

Roman held the front door open for Gisella to step out and a couple to enter the restaurant.

Raul glanced from the couple approaching the

hostess stand to his watch. "*Mierda*. Five minutes to close. I'll seat them then go warn the kitchen. Tell my mother I love her if you find my body later."

The kitchen probably did rip into Raul for not turning them away, but Shay didn't feel the usual annoyance at having a last-minute party. Even one that ordered three full courses and lingered over coffee at the end of the meal. Her mood was so bad, she didn't care.

She finally left for the night with the last of the kitchen staff, exhausted and ready for her bed. They parted ways at the cobblestone alley where her car was parked. Everyone was going for drinks, but Shay wanted nothing more than to go home and put the day behind her. There were only a few cars left, and she got to hers quickly, wasting no time putting the key in the ignition.

Silence.

"No. Come on." After multiple attempts of trying to start the car, she slapped the steering wheel with both hands and sighed out a deep breath. Time to cut her losses. She'd go back to George's and drink something strong while waiting for a cab to come. She climbed out of her car and slammed the door.

Headlights came up behind her, and she moved to the side, wrapping her arms around herself.

"Shay? Is that you?" a voice called from the slowing car.

She squinted into the beams. "Kyle?"

"Going for a late-night walk?" He pulled up next to her, taking her out of the spotlight.

"Unintentionally, yes. My car won't start."

"Want me to take a look at it? I know a little about

cars. If I can't fix it, I'll drive you home."

"Sure, thanks." Relief flooded through her. At least the end of this night was in sight.

"Hop in and show me where you parked."

"It's actually right there." She pointed to the car about twenty feet behind them.

He reversed and stepped out of his car. Taking her keys, he tried to start it with the same non-results, then popped the hood.

He used a small flashlight from his glove compartment to scan the engine, then smiled. "There. I think one of your battery cables is loose. Did you hit any bumps today?"

"This whole road is a bump," she said, cautiously optimistic that it could be something so simple.

He reattached it and told her to try the ignition again. The engine roared to life, and he closed the hood with a triumphant grin. He walked over to her driver's side door, and she rolled down the window. She couldn't have hidden her happiness if she'd tried.

"Thanks. You really saved me. It's been a bad day."

"Well, you can pay me back by letting me take you to dinner."

"For me to pay you back, you're going to take me to dinner? Sure. Why not?" She laughed, so relieved the car was running.

"That's not the most enthusiastic response I've gotten, but I'll take it. When are you free?"

"I have tomorrow night off."

"Great. I'll pick you up at your house at seven." He sauntered back to his Lexus and slid inside.

She called after him, "Do you need my address?"

He smiled confidently. "Don't worry, I'll find you."

For the second time that night, goosebumps cascaded from the base of her neck down her arms. This time, the sensation had none of the warmth Roman's had given her. Instead, it was accompanied by sudden regret for agreeing to the date.

Chapter 5

Roman

Roman came close to resting his head on the pristine white tablecloth during what felt like the fiftieth speech of the night. The only thing that kept him from actually doing it was remembering he was a grown man of twenty-eight who'd willingly agreed to give up his night in the name of charity. Instead of acting like a six-year-old, he leaned back to catch the waiter's attention and ordered another beer.

He hated these things. He wouldn't do it for anyone but Gisella. She may travel the world, and sometimes they wouldn't speak for months at a time, but she always came back. She never left for good, and she never forgot about him. It meant more to him than even Gisella probably fully understood.

Roman's mom had left when he was almost too little to remember her. There was no explanation that would have made it easy, but at least if there was drug addiction or a mental disorder it wouldn't be completely her fault. Unfortunately, she was perfectly healthy. She simply saw greener grass. The man she'd left Roman and his father for had the only thing that they did not: money. She married him as soon as the divorce was finalized and had a baby boy within a year. A baby she decided to stay with and raise.

His dad had been so devastated that he uprooted their whole life in Colombia to move to America. Once there, he took a job at an exclusive resort as the head groundskeeper. However, he was much more than a groundskeeper; he was an artist with flowers and won numerous awards in his twenty-year career. A few years ago, when he died of a sudden heart attack, Roman found a picture of his mom still tucked within the folds of his wallet. It stung.

Roman didn't need psychotherapy to realize his mom's abandonment was the reason he kept things superficial with women. It hadn't bothered him until he met Shay. He was drawn to her in a way he'd never experienced before. From the first time he'd laid eyes on her, something in him recognized she was different.

Shay.

He couldn't keep her from his thoughts if he wanted to.

He took a long drink from his beer as the next, and hopefully last speaker started their monologue. Leaning toward Gisella, he whispered, "Tell me he's the last one."

She kept a smile plastered on her face. "God, I hope so."

Ten minutes later, the speaker stepped away from the podium to a round of applause. Gisella stood, still clapping, and motioned for Roman to follow her. Discreetly, they made their way through the sea of tables, with an occasional nod toward a familiar face. When they reached the front door, Gisella practically ran down the steps to the sidewalk.

"Finally. I'm starving. Why do they serve bird food at these things?" She waved to the first in a line of cabs, then beelined toward it when the driver nodded.

Roman pulled the door open for her to glide in. "I wouldn't exactly call a four-course meal bird food."

"Valentino's on Main, please," Gisella directed the driver, then turned back to Roman. "One, salad doesn't count as a course, and two, sorbet and fruit will never count as a dessert in my book. Plus, I'm retiring from modeling, I can eat whatever I want now."

Roman laughed.

"What?" she asked.

"I've seen you dip fries in a chocolate shake for a snack. If that was restraint, I'm afraid of what's coming."

"Shut up." She slapped his arm.

A few minutes later, the cab pulled up to their go-to pizza spot. By the time Roman had paid the cabbie, Gisella was already inside seated at a booth and loosening the straps on her shoes. Roman slid into the seat across from her and leaned his elbows on the red and white checkered tablecloth.

A server approached, and Gisella happily greeted him, not wasting any time before placing their usual order. "We'll have a large pepperoni and a half carafe of house red. Thank you."

The server returned a few minutes later with the wine and some breadsticks. Gisella held the basket toward Roman first. He shook his head as he poured them each a glass.

She took a breadstick and leaned back. "Mmm. This is magic. How do they make these so good?"

"Asiago in the dough." Roman had managed to almost perfectly replicate the recipe at home.

"All right, super-chef. How much longer are you

going to let George take credit for your impeccable palate?"

"A little while, at least." Roman shifted in his seat.

"Don't you want your own place?"

"Of course. But for now, I'm good." He toyed with the stem of his wine glass, avoiding eye contact.

Gisella took a deep breath. "Is Shay part of the reason you're so content to stand still?"

There it was. This had been coming from the second Gisella's eyes lit up when she met Shay. He had intentionally asked Gisella to wait outside to avoid their paths crossing. That hadn't happened. There was an unspoken agreement between himself and Gisella— they did not talk about their dating lives. She'd never pushed those boundaries before.

"There's nothing going on between us."

"But you want there to be?" She raised her eyes over the rim of her glass as she took a sip.

"Gisella, leave it alone."

"Sorry, but how could I not be curious? You never mention any girl by name, and I've heard *Shay* come up more times than I can count over the past few months. I wanted to put a face to a name. She's very pretty."

"Oh. My. God. Drop it. I asked her out, and she turned me down. Shay and I are friends." The truth was painful to admit, especially to Gisella.

Gisella paused for a moment and gently twirled her glass, the wine trailing in a slow circle around the sides. "Well, then she has beauty and no brains. You're a catch."

Classic Gisella, pushing him to the edge then making him remember she had his back no matter what. He sighed. "You have to say that. You're my sister."

Technically, half-sister from their dad's first marriage, but truthfully Gisella had been more of a mom to him than his own mother had.

She shrugged and slid her glass out of the way to make room for the arriving pizza. "I wouldn't lie."

It was delivered by Valentino himself, and he joined them for a glass of wine as they ate. His presence kept the conversation from returning to Shay, and Roman tipped even more than he usually did when the bill arrived.

Roman pointed to what was left of the pizza. "You want a to-go box?"

She looked horrified that he'd even asked. "Of course. That's breakfast."

Roman shook his head and asked the waiter for a box. As they walked out, Gisella slipped her arm around his back. "Thank you for coming with me tonight."

"Anytime." He slung an arm over her shoulder and squeezed her to him as they walked back to his apartment.

****

During prep the next morning, Roman's mind wandered to the conversation with Gisella. He'd be lying to himself if he pretended Shay wasn't the driving force behind his continuing at George's. It shouldn't matter. He would sink or soar when he went out on his own, whether it was tomorrow or when Shay was ready to pursue her jewelry business full time.

Shay walked into the kitchen with a barely touched plate and held it out to the cook working the grill station. "I don't know what to tell you, Ricky. He says the burger is still undercooked."

Ricky tossed the tongs in his hand to the side and picked the burger up off the plate. He tore it in half and held it out toward Roman. "The guy asked for 'well.' Tell me, how much more 'well' it could get?"

Roman took it and pitched the whole plate into a bus bucket. The burger was as fully cooked as it gets. "Don't sweat it. The customer's always right, even if he's an asshole. Grill him up a hockey puck and move on."

Ricky was the newest cook on the line. He'd started as a busboy at sixteen, but Roman had gradually moved him up the chain after he saw how passionate and eager he was to learn.

"You got it, Chef." Ricky turned back to the grill looking less discouraged, put a new patty on to cook, and pressed it down with a spatula.

Across the line, Shay was looking at her phone, her eyebrows knit together.

"Bad news?" Roman asked.

"What? No—"

The door to the walk-in fridge flung open, cutting her off. Alex stepped out carrying a bucket full of limes. He walked up to Shay and read over her shoulder. "*Pick you up at seven. 426 Willow Lane.* Would that happen to be a certain admirer I noticed last night at the bar?"

"Yeah, he wore me down, but I'm reconsidering." She had barely started to type a reply when Alex snatched the phone from her hand. "Hey, Alex. What are you doing?"

"Saving you from yourself. There, done." He handed the phone back to her.

She glanced at the message he'd sent.

—Can't wait.—

Shay stared at him. "You know I was about to cancel. Now, I'm going to look insane when I tell him I changed my mind."

"So, don't cancel." Alex picked up his limes and left.

Shay scowled at her phone.

Roman gripped the edge of the counter between him and Shay. "Cancel. Let me take you out." No smoothing it out, no flirting. He just put it out there.

"Roman, you can't expect—"

This time, Ricky cut her off. "One rock on a bun for table go-screw-yourself." He thrust the plate across the line. Shay picked it up, not finishing what she was about to say.

Roman ran a hand over his short hair. He grabbed the kitchen towel that was slung over his shoulder and snapped it down to the counter to scrub at a stain.

Shay's turning him down hurt, but it was going to kill him knowing she was out with some other guy. He had no right to feel so territorial. They weren't dating. He just didn't understand why not. She liked him. He saw it every time she looked at him. Until now, he thought she was guarded against dating anyone. But she was willing to go out with this guy she barely knew. The closest Roman had gotten was what he considered pre-dates on the loading dock.

He entered the walk-in refrigerator to take inventory, hoping the cold air would snap him out of the foul mood he'd plowed into headfirst. It didn't work, and his thoughts stayed on Shay.

****

Her birthday should have at least counted as a date.

It had been a beautiful night, warm with a breeze. Late enough that the city had started to quiet when he led her out to the loading dock and lit the candle on the waiting cupcake.

"Happy birthday," he'd said, holding it toward her.

She'd worn an expression of pure surprise. "Roman…How did you know?"

"The night you left your wallet on the bar, I may have peeked at your ID. Here. Make a wish."

She looked up at him for a second then pursed her lips and blew out the candle. He handed her the cupcake and gestured to the pallets he'd piled up for seats.

"Come, enjoy your birthday in style." Part of him expected her to laugh and go back inside, but she didn't. A jolt of happiness hit him when she sat down and took a bite of the cupcake.

"This is great. Janet made it?" She licked frosting off her finger and took another bite.

"Nah, I brought it in. It seemed like you weren't advertising that it was your birthday today, so I didn't want to call attention to it."

She nodded. "Thanks. Want a bite?"

"No, I'm good." He was. He'd eaten three earlier and still had half a dozen of the batch he'd made waiting at home. "So, is it all holidays you go low-key, or just your birthday?"

She took another bite of the cupcake and leaned against the wall behind her. "Pretty much all holidays."

"Your family wasn't big on celebrations?"

"They were, but it was just me and my parents. They died in a car wreck when I was fifteen, and I rode out the rest of my teens in a foster home."

Her revelation struck him. Growing up, he'd known what it was like to lose one parent, but his dad was as solid as granite. Shay had no one as far as he could tell. "I'm sorry," he said, "about your parents, I mean."

"Thanks. I lucked out compared to some stories I've heard. The home I got placed in wasn't bad at all. There were a lot of us, so birthdays were usually something simple. I started to really like simple." She held up the empty cupcake wrapper. "Like this."

"Good. I'm really glad I didn't go the surprise party route now."

Shay laughed. "I would have died of embarrassment. This is perfect."

****

It had been perfect. And now, she was on her way to have a perfect night with some trust-fund kid who would try to sweep her off her feet. That thought alone was enough to send Roman running after her when he caught sight of her leaving after the lunch rush.

"Shay, wait." He jogged across the dining room and caught up to her at the bar.

"What's up?" She turned to him with a blank look.

He took a deep breath. "I meant it earlier. Cancel with moneybags and give me a chance."

"We're better as friends, Roman." She looked away and bit her lip. The same tell she had when they played card games on slow nights. She was lying.

"We're great as friends. I think we could be a lot more." He tilted his head to catch her gaze.

"Yeah? Even if I was okay in a one-of-many situation, what happens when it doesn't work out? We'd still have to come to work and see each other

46

every day. I need this job."

"You wouldn't be one-of-many, and you won't lose your job. I've dated plenty of people I've worked with." *Oh, fuck.* He couldn't have picked a worse thing to say.

She pinched her lips together against whatever she'd been about to say. Instead, she looked down at her phone. "I've gotta go. I'll see you tomorrow."

There was nothing to do but watch her leave and regret all the things he should have said. *You won't have to worry about it because we won't break up. None of those girls mattered an ounce as much as you do to me. I think I'm falling in love with you.*

Roman clenched his jaw. Hopefully, this lucky stranger would have no personality underneath his hair gel, and he'd get another chance to change her mind.

Chapter 6

Shay

Shay had never been so glad that she hadn't sent a text in her life. She'd made up her mind to cancel on Kyle when Roman caught up to her. After their conversation, she deleted the message backing out of the date. A night with a charming distraction was exactly what she needed.

Roman seemed to think that it was somehow his place to tell her not to go out with someone. Meanwhile, he had what was becoming a full-blown girlfriend who, *literally,* stepped off the pages of a Victoria's Secret catalogue. Unbelievable.

Shay ran a brush through her already combed hair and stared at herself in the full-length mirror in her bedroom. The anger written across her face distracted from the short black dress and strappy heels she'd pulled out since she now had an incentive for this date to go well. That wouldn't happen if she kept scowling.

It didn't help that she still felt apprehensive in general about the evening. When Kyle had texted her the correct address, it creeped her out. The night he'd fixed her car, he told her he'd find her, but she expected an internet search would give him her old address. She'd only moved a month ago and hadn't even forwarded her mail yet since all her bills were electronic.

It bothered her even more that she'd spent her ten-minute break today searching for herself on the internet and never once did any search link her to her current address. He'd found it somehow though. Maybe rich people had a more powerful search engine.

She touched up her lipstick as a knock sounded on her front door.

Standing on the front porch, Kyle looked even more polished than he had at brunch. He wore a tailored navy suit and seemed almost airbrushed, with gelled hair and not one visible pore on his flawless face. His wide mouth spread ear to ear in a grin when she opened the door.

"Wow. Just wow." He looked her up and down. "Here. These are for you."

She took the bouquet of twelve long-stemmed, pale-pink roses. "Thank you. They're beautiful. I'll put them in water and be right back." She ducked inside to fill a tall glass with water and took a deep breath. *Here we go.*

When she joined him on the porch, he still looked like he had an inside joke. "You really look amazing. You're going to look even better in my play car."

He put a hand on her lower back and guided her down the stairs toward a sleek red Ferrari. Inside, the smell of his sharp cologne was overpowering. That, along with him doubling the speed limit on the highway, had Shay carsick by the time they pulled up to The Cliffside, one of the most exclusive restaurants in the state.

Her hand was on the door handle even before they came to a jerking stop and once out of the car, she greedily gulped lungsful of air, cool from the breeze off the ocean. It helped, and the queasy feeling dissipated, soon replaced by hunger.

Kyle handed his keys to the valet and held out an arm for her. "Shall we?"

She hooked her arm through, and he squeezed his elbow in, pinning her arm against the taut muscles beneath his jacket.

A few couples and groups were inside waiting to be seated. Kyle led her past them, and they entered a nearly all-white dining room. Tables were set with china, and massive windows spread around three sides of the room letting in a spectacular view of the ocean below.

A maître d' rushed through the nearly full dining room to greet them. "Good evening, Mr. Matthews. I didn't know you would be dining with us this evening."

"I'm sure you'll find somewhere to put us, William." Kyle held out a discretely folded bill which William took.

"Of course. Right this way."

"Good man." Kyle gestured for Shay to follow first as William led them to a table against one of the windows.

After William saw them to their seats, he snapped his fingers for a server to come, making Shay cringe. This was the type of place she would never consider working. The staff at George's joked about being overly pretentious, but the food was amazing, the managers treated employees like family, and everyone was respected.

A waiter arrived with menus. "Good evening. The sommelier will be over momentarily. Would you like something to drink in the meanwhile?"

Kyle kept his gaze on Shay. "No need for the sommelier. I know what I want." If he was going for flirty, he'd overshot into predatory. She resisted the urge to glance at her phone for a time check. This was going to be a long night.

"We'll start with a bottle of your best champagne and oysters on the half shell." He shook his head when Shay started to tell him she didn't like oysters. "Trust me. You'll love it."

"Right away, sir. Fresh baked rolls will be over momentarily."

"No, thanks." He turned to Shay. "We don't need the carbs."

Her rumbling stomach would have killed for a carb. When the oysters came, she tried one out of desperation. Still not her thing. She replaced the empty shell on the dish and took a sip of champagne. It was delicious, but with nothing in her stomach, she switched to water.

The waiter returned and Kyle ordered two steaks, rare.

"I'd like mine medium," Shay cut in.

"No, trust me. This is some of the best meat you've ever tasted. You don't want to ruin it." Looking at the waiter he reiterated, "Rare." The waiter gave her an apologetic look before he left.

When the steaks came, Shay took a few bites and was about to send hers back when Kyle commented on the fact that she'd only been eating around the more cooked edges. "I like that you're a picky eater. You only need to lose like five pounds, and you'll be a ten."

Shay almost dropped her fork. *What. The. Fuck.*

She cut a huge piece and proceeded to eat all but the rarest portion in the very center, then excused herself to the bathroom. With no chance he would order dessert if he was that concerned about her weight, the date could finally be over. She couldn't stand another minute of the onslaught of name drops and casual references to his wealth that had dominated the dinner conversation. Any chance of him charming her had completely disintegrated.

She returned to the table, hoping he'd finished his food and they could leave. As she came closer, she saw their plates were cleared, but two snifters of amber liquid were waiting in their place. Kyle had leaned back, sipping his, and staring out across the ocean. It looked like a staged photo from a magazine she would never buy.

When she sat, he turned to face her. "I ordered a nightcap. I guarantee it'll have you enjoying the rest of your night. This brandy is over eight-hundred dollars a bottle. I'm sure you've never tasted anything like it." He sniffed his own glass as the waiter pushed in her chair. She took a small sip. He was right—it was delicious. Smooth and complex, it warmed her all the way to her toes.

"It's really good," she admitted. *Probably the highlight of the night in fact.*

His attention was caught by someone over her shoulder. "Good. Drink up. I'll be right back." He slid out of his seat, and Shay turned to see him greeting a group of older, well-dressed men who had arrived at a nearby table. She settled back into her chair, looking out the window to where the sunset reflected off the clouds over the water.

Their waiter came over to refill her water. With her glass midway to her lips for her second sip she paused as he breathed out a warning, "I think he put something in your drink." Without a glance at Shay, he was gone.

Sitting up straight, she held the glass up to the light of the setting sun and swirled the liquid. At the very bottom, tiny little flecks of white stirred to life. *That bastard.*

In one motion, she grabbed her purse and stood, almost tipping over her chair. Across the room, Kyle turned in her direction and frowned. He took long strides to cut her off before she could get very far.

"Get out of my way," she said through gritted teeth.

"What's the hurry? If you're ready to go, I'll settle the bill and take you home. No need to rush."

"Why's that? So whatever you put in my drink has time to work?"

All traces of good humor vanished, replaced by the same spark of rage that she'd caught a glimpse of when she first turned him down.

"I didn't put anything in your drink."

The fury in his eyes sent a chill down Shay's spine.

She shook it off and stood her ground. "Well, I don't think eight-hundred-dollar brandy should have white chunks floating around in it. You should probably have them take it off the bill. Goodnight."

She tried to walk past him, but he side-stepped farther into her path and put one hand on her arm, gripping harder than he needed to.

"I already told you. I didn't put anything in your drink." His fingers tightened causing her to gasp and look up to meet his angry stare. "But I did buy you a meal worth more than you make in a week, so let's sit back down. I'll order you another drink, and we can have a nice end to the night."

"There's no way that's happening. This is done. Move." He didn't budge, and she played the only card she had. "Let me go, or I'll make a scene in front of all your fancy friends here."

"Make more of a scene than you already have, and I will ruin you, bitch." He smiled through clenched teeth. She could feel his heartbeat through his palm where it gripped her arm like a vise. "Now, calm the fuck down." Kyle smiled and nodded to a couple nearby.

Shay tried to shake off his hand, but he held tight.

Play dead. "Fine," she agreed, taking a deep breath.

He smoothed his hair back and led the way back to their table, keeping his grip on her arm even when he pulled out her chair. With her free hand, she picked up her glass and flung the liquid at his face, aiming for his eyes. He staggered back stunned, and she yanked her arm away.

Not wasting a second glance at him, she turned and left as fast as she could in heels. She raced out of the restaurant and past the valet. She zigzagged a couple of blocks away before stopping and pulling out her phone to order a car.

When the car arrived, she sank into the worn seat, relieved that the night was over. In twenty minutes, she would be home. "Could you take the back way to Portland?" She didn't want to risk running into Kyle by driving on main roads.

"Sure thing, miss. Scenic route it is." They pulled away from the curb, and she let her head rest back against the seat.

The driver turned onto what used to pass as a highway. Now it was a two-way street running alongside the multi-lane freeway. Bright lights flooded the inside of the cab as a car sped up behind them, only slowing inches from hitting them. Shay's heart pounded. *Kyle.*

"What's this guy's problem?" The cab driver kept a steady speed as the car swerved into the other lane and pulled up next to them. There was no mistaking Kyle's car as it lunged forward and cut them off before slowing to a crawl.

"This guy's a fucking lunatic," the driver swore as he pulled into the left lane to pass him. Next to them, Kyle sped up, matching their speed. There was no way they could reenter the right lane. Ahead, headlights flickered into existence as a car rounded a curve and headed straight toward them.

"Oh my God. Pull over," Shay yelled as the lights approached rapidly.

"There's no shoulder here." The cab driver's voice echoed her terror. "Hold on!" he yelled back at her, then slammed on his brakes and swerved into the correct lane before Kyle had a chance to react. They came to a dead stop. Not twenty feet ahead Kyle's tires screeched as he skidded to a stop. The oncoming car passed, honking.

At least a minute went by while they waited. Shay's heart thundered against her ribs the entire time. Finally, Kyle gunned his engine and shot forward out of view.

"Are you okay?" The cab driver looked at her through the rearview mirror. His chest heaved as he tried to catch his breath.

She nodded, and he took a deep breath.

"I'm going to call the police." He fumbled, picking up his phone from the cup holder next to him.

"We should go. In case he comes back." Shay's voice shook.

The driver dialed 911 and drove as he spoke to the operator. Shay didn't correct him when he stammered out that neither of them noticed the make of the car. Something told her reporting Kyle would only pull him back into her life. If she learned nothing else from tonight, it was that she wanted nothing to do with Kyle Matthews.

She pulled out her phone about ten times on the drive, debating on calling Alex to see if she could stay over. Then a better thought occurred to her, and she called her upstairs neighbor, Henry, instead.

When they pulled up in front of her apartment, Shay tipped the driver twice the fare and went straight upstairs. The seventy-year-old former boxer opened the door. Between his legs, the reason Shay was there poked his furry head out.

Shay knelt down as the pit bull licked her face. "Hi, Bear. You wanna come have a sleepover?"

Henry chuckled. "You bet he does. Anything for some attention." More seriously, he asked her, "Everything okay?"

Shay stood and faced the older man. "Yeah. I had a bad date and would feel a little better with some company tonight." She scratched behind Bear's ears, and he leaned all ninety pounds of himself into her leg.

"You couldn't pick a better companion. He may be a mushy lump with the people he likes, but if anyone bothers you, he'll go for their throat."

"Well, thanks for letting me borrow him. I'll walk him before I bring him back tomorrow."

"Anytime." He held out a leash and a baggie of dog food. "Breakfast."

Shay thanked him again and led Bear back down to her apartment.

Between the adrenaline rush crashing and barely eating dinner, she was famished. She ordered a pizza, triple-checked her doors and windows were locked, plugged her phone in to charge, and stepped into a hot shower to wash off any remnants of Kyle's cologne before the food arrived.

****

The next morning, Shay intentionally slept in. There was no way in hell she was going out of her way for GG's coffee ever again. She'd get used to the drip coffee brewed for employees at George's, or the watered-down version of her usual favorite from the campus café.

After she dropped Bear off, she looked at her phone as she walked to her car and saw she'd missed a text from the night before. It was a link from Kyle.

She hesitated, hovering her finger over it before tapping the screen. It was a meme with the words "Sleep tight, Shay" superimposed over the Valentino's logo.

Her blood went cold. That's where she'd ordered from last night. Backtracking to the time-stamped message, it was sent around the same time her pizza had arrived. He'd been sitting outside watching. It made her skin crawl, and she glanced around but saw no sign of him now. She drove straight to the police station to file a report.

It went better than she expected. The officer not only took her statement but also asked if she would come back the following day to meet with a detective. Knowing they took it seriously made her feel better.

She was too late to drop off a fresh batch of earrings to the boutique that had requested more, but on time for her dinner shift at St. George's. She pulled a clean shirt off the uniform rack and hung it on her open locker as the door to the locker room opened behind her.

Chapter 7

Roman

Roman walked into the locker room with Alex. Shay was getting ready, and he planned to rush out before she said anything he didn't want to hear to about her date.

"Well, hello there," Alex purred at Shay. "It better be slow, because I need all the details from last night. Are you going to have his babies?"

"No way in hell. He was awful." She kept her head down as she pulled off her sweatshirt, exposing a tank-top underneath.

Roman perked up. "Of course, he was awful when you have me to compare him to. Stop trying to make me jealous with other men and just agree to marry me." *Please.* He swung his chef jacket on and popped the collar.

Alex narrowed his eyes in Roman's direction. "Oh, simmer down, Mr. Jealousy. You have a new girlfriend coming in here every week."

It wasn't a completely incorrect statement. He'd dated a couple of girls the first month Shay started but soon realized there was no point. Whoever he was with, he wished it was Shay. It wasn't fun, and it wasn't fair to the girls. Roman couldn't help the edge of annoyance in his voice. "Every week? Not for a long time. The only woman I've been out with in months is Gisella."

Alex cocked his head. "Oh, right, *just* Gisella. How silly of me."

Snapping his head back to Shay, Alex drew out his next word. "Anyway...How awful are we talking? Poor hygiene bad, or talked about his mommy issues all night bad? Because, honestly, I think we can make either situation work."

Shay picked up the hanger with her work shirt and answered without turning around. "Like he's psychotic and drugged my drink bad."

When she turned, Roman caught sight of her bare arm. Dark bruises circled her bicep. He stiffened, frozen in place by the wave of anger that cascaded through him.

Alex rushed to her and gently lifted her arm to inspect it. "Oh my God. You aren't joking, are you? Are you okay?"

"I'm fine. *Really.*" She pulled her arm away.

Across the room, Roman couldn't take his eyes off the bruise, and his fingernails dug into his palms. He practically growled out the question that was playing on a loop in his mind. "What's his fucking name?"

Shay turned to him, uncharacteristic dark circles under her eyes. "His name doesn't matter. I want the whole thing left alone." She pulled on her work shirt and began to button it up.

"I'm so sorry I pushed you toward him," Alex told her. He sat on the bench in the middle of the room and ran a hand through his hair. "I thought it was romantic when he showed up here Tuesday night to ask you out a second time."

"Nope, not romantic. His friends wanted to stop

here for a drink before going to dinner somewhere else. He just happened to see me."

"False. He was here alone." Alex looked up at her. "He came in by himself and bought rounds for the group next to him, but they were coworkers, out for happy hour. I'm positive he didn't know them before he started buying them drinks. He left right after you agreed to go out with him. Alone."

"I didn't agree. I turned him down again." Shay's brow furrowed.

"So…wait…when did you agree?" Alex asked.

"It was later, after my shift. I ran into him when my car wouldn't start. He fixed it, so I said I'd go."

Roman's heart pounded. "What was wrong with your car?"

"One of the battery cables came off."

Roman did his best to not grit his teeth, but his jaw wouldn't unclench. "If that had happened by accident, the car would have shut off while you were driving it. He probably set it up himself so he would look like a hero. He's stalking you."

"You need to go to the police," Alex said quickly.

"I did, this morning to report the drugs and to show them this." She handed her phone to Alex with the text from Kyle on the screen. "Click the link."

Alex tapped the screen, and the meme opened. "He's a Valentino's fan?"

"That's where I ordered from when I got home. I think he was watching my house because he sent this right around the time my pizza was delivered. I have a meeting with a detective tomorrow at three."

Roman stepped behind Alex and looked over his shoulder. He was about to reach for the phone to look at it closer when Shay took it back.

"Holy shit." Alex crossed his arms in front of his chest. "You're staying with me until he's arrested, or at least until you have a restraining order against him."

"Isn't your roommate's brother already staying on your couch?" she asked.

"Yes. Crap. Good point. I'll get a bag after work and stay at your house then."

"Thanks, Alex, but you don't need to do that."

"Someone does," Roman said. "You can't stay alone." The thought of Kyle coming within a mile of her had his stomach churning.

"It'll be fun. We'll catch up on trash TV." Alex wrapped one arm around her and pulled her in for a half-hug.

She rolled her eyes. "Fine. Yes."

Roman's shoulders relaxed. If she refused to let someone stay with her, she was going to have one pissed-off sous chef on her porch in a sleeping bag until this guy was arrested.

Relief flooded through Alex's words. "Good. Don't eat before you leave. It'll be Thai and Tequila all night."

Roman turned to face his locker. He busied himself, emptying pockets that didn't need to be emptied to keep from giving in to the overwhelming urge to pull her to him as she walked by.

Shay walked out, and Roman turned to where Alex had slumped on the bench.

He shook his head and glanced at Roman. "I fucking pushed her to go out with him. I didn't even catch the creep vibe."

Roman let the silence hang between them for a

moment before he cleared his throat. "If you see that piece of shit here or anywhere near her house, you call the police, then you call me. What's his name?"

Alex didn't hesitate. "Kyle Matthews. His dad is senator Jack Matthews."

"Thank you for that. And thank you for staying with her." Roman walked out and went to the kitchen. He recognized the feeling burning a hole in his gut, the same helpless anger he'd felt two years ago when Gisella was attacked.

It wasn't a surprise some amount of unwanted attention came with Gisella's success. She'd entered the spotlight when she was still a teenager living in Colombia, and there had been a few fans over the years who took it farther than comfortable. Once in a while, a threatening email or letter would show up.

Nothing had prepared either her or Roman for the night an obsessed fan broke into her house. By luck, Roman happened to be visiting and was home, upstairs. She'd come in late, and Roman was already asleep when her terrified screams echoed through the house.

The guy got much more than he expected, including jail time, a restraining order, and his jaw wired shut after Roman pulled him off Gisella. One of the worst parts was Gisella apologizing after the police hauled the guy away. As if she had somehow brought it on herself. It still pissed him off to think about it.

Since that night, they'd done everything he could think of to keep it from happening again. Gisella installed state-of-the-art security systems at her apartments in LA and France, and her house in Colombia. Roman did the same at his apartment for when she visited. She also hired bodyguards for all public events from that point on. Any time she got some particularly unwanted attention, she upped the bodyguards to twenty-four hours a day until the person was found and deterred.

A threat to someone he loved was one of the only things that brought out Roman's temper. The thought of what could've happened if Kyle had succeeded in drugging Shay pushed him over the edge. He pulled out his phone and looked up Kyle Matthews. Within minutes he'd burned the guy's image into his brain.

Even though it was busy, the night dragged. The only breaths of relief Roman got from his simmering anger were when Shay came into the kitchen. She looked better as the night went on. Less preoccupied.

He ducked out, down to the loading dock on his break. On his phone, he pulled up the contact info for Gisella's current bodyguard, Pete. Roman had met him a few times, and they'd gotten along. Hopefully, Pete would be up for a favor.

"Hello."

"Hey, this is Roman."

"I know, man. What's up?"

"I have a favor to ask."

"Shoot."

"There's a guy bothering a waitress I work with."

"Shay?"

Oh, fuck. If Gisella had mentioned Shay to her bodyguard, she probably wasn't going to be dropping the subject anytime soon.

"Yeah, Shay. I need the guy's address. I can't find anything local when I search. I was hoping with your background, you may be able to dig something up." Roman had read Pete's resume and had no doubt from his history as a hacker in a Special Forces unit that he could dig up the launch codes for nukes if he wanted to.

"No problem. Name?"

"Kyle Matthews. His dad's a senator, Jack Matthews."

"Fun. I'll hit you back soon."

"Thanks."

He'd finally started to relax, knowing Pete would help him.

The evening rush began to die down, and Shay came to get bread for a table. Roman's mood improved even more when he heard her laugh with one of the other servers.

The door to the kitchen swung open, and the hostess rushed in. The frown she wore usually meant she knew she was about to piss off someone with bad news.

Glancing around, her eyes landed on Shay at the far end of the kitchen. "Shay?"

"Don't even, Terri. I'm done for the night. Don't tell me you sat me."

"I'm sorry. They asked for you specifically. The guy was insistent."

Shay's head snapped toward Roman. The flash of fear in her eyes was all the incentive he needed. He tossed down the bowl in his hands and jogged out of the kitchen.

Kyle wasn't hard to pick out sitting at a table against the back wall of the room. The cocky piece of crap was leaning back in his chair across from a blonde who was busy taking selfies. When Shay entered the dining room, his smug expression turned into a wide smile.

Roman took long strides across the room, ignoring Shay's whispered calls to stop. She was terrified, and this guy had the nerve to sit there, amused. Roman increased his pace. That smile would be gone in a minute.

He plowed past tables until he reached Kyle's, stopping himself short of yanking him out of his chair. "Get up," Roman growled through gritted teeth.

"What's this?" Kyle's eyes sparkled. "Are you here to take our drink order?"

"I'm here to kick your rapist ass. Now, get up, and get outside."

Humor gone, Kyle frowned. Nearby tables had gone silent, and his date stared at him in confusion. Kyle calmly folded his napkin and stood.

"Yeah, I'm not going to do that, so why don't you get back to washing dishes." He moved closer to Roman and whispered, "And that stupid whore should be so lucky to have me rape her. Maybe she still will."

The final word was barely out of his mouth when Roman slammed him into the wall with one hand on his throat. "You want to harass someone, come after me, and see where it gets you, you piece of shit."

Raul came out of nowhere and put one hand on Roman's arm. "Let him go."

Roman's eyes didn't leave Kyle's, and he grit his teeth. "Don't you ever threaten her again."

Kyle's face turned from red to a deep purple.

"Roman, now!" Raul barked. Roman let go, and Kyle dropped to the floor gasping for air.

"You'll pay for that," Kyle snarled. He got to his feet and snapped at his date to get up. She trailed behind him as he strode out of the dining room with his head down.

Raul stepped back from Roman. "Get in my office."

Roman didn't argue, and Alex motioned quiet applause as Roman passed the bar, following Raul.

It was a formality. He was fired. He just hoped Kyle was stupid enough to be waiting for him outside.

Chapter 8

Shay

Shay's feet wouldn't move. This couldn't be happening. *Roman was going to get fired.* The thought snapped her out of her shock, and she rushed to Raul's office. When she entered, Raul was pacing and yelling at Roman.

"Just go home. I don't know what I can do from here." Raul sank into his desk chair and waved him away.

"Fine." Roman turned to leave. His gaze landed on Shay for a second. He didn't say anything but squeezed her shoulder as he passed by.

"Roman, wait." She tried to stop him, but he didn't turn back.

Her head swiveled toward Raul. "Raul, please. That guy is stalking me. Roman knows and was only trying to help me."

"Shay, go back to work." He sighed, slumping over his desk. "I'll talk to George, but he's not going to let any employee make a scene like that and still work here."

"Please try. Tell him it won't happen again," she begged.

Raul nodded and frowned as he shooed her out with a wave. "Go."

She rushed straight back to the locker room, where Roman was shutting his now empty locker. A full backpack rested on the ground next to him.

The composure she'd barely hung onto over the past twenty-four hours crumbled, and tears filled her eyes.

Roman turned to her and shook his head. "Don't cry." He crossed the space between them and folded his arms around her.

"I'm so sorry." She melted into his sturdy chest. He'd changed into a T-shirt and smelled fresh, like soap and aftershave.

"Hey." He pulled away enough that she could look into his eyes. "You have nothing to be sorry for. That scumbag put his hands on you, threatened you, and showed up at your job to harass you. He's the one who'll be sorry."

"Roman, you're probably losing your job." She pulled away and composed herself, determined not to fall completely apart in front of him.

He reached back to pick up his bag. "Eh, I was over it. Time for bigger and better things. If you hadn't started working here, I would've left already." The playful spark was back in his eyes.

"You're unbelievable," she said, unable to suppress a smile.

"That's what I've been told." He winked as he backed out of the locker room. "See you tomorrow at three."

Her smile faded as soon as she caught his meaning. She wasn't going to drag him any farther into this mess by having him come to her meeting with the detective. "Roman, no. You don't have to do that."

"I know I don't. But I am. Don't go anywhere alone until then. Promise?" He didn't walk away until she nodded agreement.

He peered into the kitchen on his way by. "*Adios, pendejos!*" His goodbye was met with a clamor of cheers and banging pots and pans as the staff showed their support for him. Word had spread fast about what had happened.

Shay wiped her eyes and took a deep breath before walking back to the dining room where other servers had seamlessly covered her tables.

****

The next afternoon, when Shay got into Alex's car to go to the police station, she was acutely aware that he was also being put out by her current situation. "If Roman isn't there, just drop me off. I'll be okay."

"First of all, no. Secondly, you don't have to worry about it, because I can promise he'll be there. That guy has it bad for you."

"He doesn't. We're friends."

Alex's eyebrows shot up toward his hairline as he looked over at her. "Please."

"Alex, have you seen his girlfriend? I think it's safe to say I'm not his type."

"I don't know," Alex said. "I see how he is with you. You may be more his type than you think."

"He flirts with all the waitresses." Shay used one of the arguments she told herself on a daily basis, trying to talk herself out of her building feelings.

"It's not the same flirting as it is with you. With you it's, I don't know, intense. It's different," he added when she looked at him incredulously. "Besides, the only other waitresses I've seen him flirt with recently are ones he'd never have a chance with."

"That's not true. I've seen him flirt with Janine. She's super nice."

"She's more into women than men."

"And Sarah."

"She's into Janine."

"Okay. Well, I've also seen him flirt with Melody."

Alex raised his eyebrows.

Shay shrugged. "What?"

"Really. Do you not follow any of the workplace drama?" His eyes lit up. "Sarah cheated on Melody with Janine and...you know what, not important. My whole point is that I think what Roman said the other day was true. He stopped seeing everyone else besides Gisella since you came."

"Oh, yes. Just Gisella, with the six-foot-long legs." Shay rolled her eyes.

Alex peered through the windshield and slowed to a stop next to the curb. "There's our Casanova now."

True to his word, Roman was outside the police station at quarter to three. He was in jeans and an untucked, blue T-shirt that matched his eyes. He jogged over and pulled open her door. "Ready, *mi cielo*?"

"So ready." She'd talked a good game, but it was a relief she didn't have to do this alone. Alex would've wanted to come in if Roman hadn't shown, but he'd have to call out of work. Under no circumstance was she costing someone else their job.

They signed in and were told Lieutenant Bask was waiting for them.

The first hitch of apprehension hit Shay. "Lieutenant? I thought I was seeing a detective?"

The officer leading them said, "It got escalated."

He pushed open the door to a conference room.

Shay's breath caught in her throat, and next to her, Roman went rigid. The lieutenant was not alone. Kyle swiveled back and forth in a chair at one end of the table. His cocky smile practically glowed, and he was surrounded by what Shay had to assume were a team of lawyers based on their suits and briefcases. Kyle pitched forward in his chair to sit up straight as his eyes flicked between Roman and her.

"Perfect." Kyle chuckled and rubbed his hands together.

"Ms. Cole." The out of shape, red-faced lieutenant stood and offered his hand. "I'm Lieutenant Bask." His attention turned to Roman. "And you are?"

"Roman Garcia."

"Roman Miguel Garcia?"

"I am," Roman said, narrowing his eyes as the door closed behind them.

"Please, sit." Lieutenant Bask gestured to the vacant chairs opposite to Kyle and cleared his throat. "I read the complaint you filed yesterday and just spoke with Mr. Matthews. It seems that, while your complaints do not warrant a restraining order, his, in fact, do."

"What?" Shay wasn't sure she heard him right. Bask held up a hand, stopping her.

"Furthermore, his legal team and I have advised him to move forward with assault and extortion charges."

"If you think what I did was assault, I'd be happy to put it in perspective." Roman directed his comment across the table at Kyle.

Kyle sat back, grinning smugly. "Smart. Threaten

me in the presence of lawyers and police. I had a feeling there wasn't an IQ requirement to wash dishes."

The lawyer next to Kyle cleared his throat and looked at Roman. "You're not being charged with assault. She is." He gestured toward Shay. "I have a room full of people who saw her throw sixty-proof alcohol directly into my client's face. He could've gone blind."

"Extortion?" Shay asked, unable to process what was unfolding.

The lawyer turned his gaze on Shay. "Yes, Ms. Cole. You texting Mr. Matthews that you would go to the police with false allegations unless he paid you five thousand dollars is in fact extortion."

"I never texted him anything."

Kyle's lawyer pulled out a piece of paper and read off a cell number. "Is that your phone number?"

"Yes," Shay said.

He slid the paper over to her. It showed a printed exchange of texts between her and Kyle, where she told him she had just filed a complaint against him which she would withdraw if he paid her. The texts were sent yesterday morning right after she left the police station.

"That's my number, but I swear I never sent these." She looked from the paper to the lawyer.

Roman took the paper from her and scrutinized it. "You could've just printed this off a computer. You want to see some actual proof of who assaulted who, look at her arm." He flung the paper down.

Kyle shook his head. "Proof of what? Any marks on her probably came from you. You've already demonstrated you're unstable and violent."

"Only a piece of shit coward puts their hands on a

woman." Roman's voice grew angrier by the second. "This is all bullshit. You're harassing her because she saw you for what you are. A lowlife not worth her time."

"You couldn't even comprehend my worth." Kyle seethed. The lawyer put a hand on Kyle's arm. Kyle yanked it away but regained composure and sat back confidently. "You don't believe I'm the one being harassed? Check her phone."

Shay pulled out her phone and opened her messages. The blood drained from her face. There, under the link to the meme Kyle had sent, was the whole conversation.

"What the hell?" she said confused. "I didn't write this. I swear." She looked to the Lieutenant first, then to Roman who'd taken her phone and was scrolling through the conversation with furrowed brows.

"Deleting it won't change anything. We can get them back from the phone company," Kyle interjected as Roman began to swipe across the screen.

"Roman." Shay willed him to believe her. "I didn't send those."

His curt reply sent a shock of dread through her. "You need a lawyer."

Lieutenant Bask motioned for the officers standing outside the door to come in. Both Shay and Roman stood.

Shay's voice shook as the officers approached. "Don't I get a phone call?"

The officers moved between Shay and Roman, forcing him to step back until they had him against a wall.

"Turn around," one commanded, opening a pair of

handcuffs.

"Unbelievable." Roman shook his head and shot an incredulous look at Lieutenant Bask. "Pretty sure you should be reading me my rights if I'm being arrested."

The officer with the handcuffs stepped closer. "You have no rights. You're not being arrested. You're being detained. At least until ICE gets here to deport your ass back to Colombia. Turn around now. Hands behind your back."

"I'm not illegal."

The officer holding the handcuffs sneered. "Sure you're not. Make sure to tell ICE."

Roman stared the officer down with a clenched jaw.

The officer looked up at him. "Oh, good, you want to do things the hard way." He kicked one of Roman's legs at the same time he twisted his arm behind his back. It sent Roman off balance, and the officer used the momentum to drive him into the wall. Roman let out a small grunt as he used his free hand to slam Shay's phone into the cinderblock wall, then drop it to the floor. He brought his heel down on the screen twice before a second officer joined the first in pressing him harder into the wall.

Shay cried out involuntarily at the rough treatment and stood to go to him.

"Stop." The lieutenant's sharp voice held her back. "Sit back down, or I'll add to your charges."

"Roman," she called, helpless as they frisked him, removing his wallet, phone, and keys from his pockets. He'd stopped resisting and made no indication that he heard her.

"You can't do this." She'd turned to the Lieutenant

to argue and heard the sound of the handcuffs clicking shut. Whipping her head back, it felt like a bad dream as she watched them lead Roman through the open door. "No! Wait!" Shay tried to follow them, but the Lieutenant blocked her way.

"I guess you didn't know your boyfriend was illegal?" Kyle's voice dripped with humor as he cupped his hands around his mouth to carry his voice and called after Roman. "Enjoy your cage."

She yelled down the hall, "Roman!"

Roman kept walking, head down, following the officers through a door at the end of the hall where he disappeared from sight.

"Sit down, Ms. Cole," Lieutenant Bask commanded.

"No. Just arrest me," she spat out.

Kyle looked up from where he'd been absently scrolling through his cell phone. "This has been fun, but I don't think I'll be pressing charges. Just give her the restraining order."

His lawyer tried to stop him, emphasizing that extortion wasn't something he should just let go, but he refused.

"I think she learned her lesson. There's no point coming after me." He stood and leaned across the table toward her. Every muscle in her body tensed. "I always get what I want in the end." He straightened back up and smoothed out his shirt. "Have a nice life, Shay."

Lieutenant Bask opened a folder and pulled out a piece of paper from which he read the terms the restraining order.

"No contact by phone, text, email, or in person. Stay at least one thousand feet from Mr. Matthews at all times. Penalty for violation is immediate arrest. Mr. Matthews has provided a list of places he frequents." He handed her the list.

"How do I know when he's going to be at any one of these places?" It listed over fifty locations including GG's coffee shop and George's.

"You can't. Your best bet is to avoid them."

"The restaurant I work at is on here. He can't make me quit my job, can he?"

The Lieutenant shrugged. "It's on the list."

Panic set in. "Can I fight this?"

He looked genuinely sorry for her. "You can, but you won't win. To get the restraining order, he provided three separate affidavits from witnesses who saw you attack him."

"I was trying to get away from him. None of the witnesses said anything about him grabbing me?"

"They did not." Bask tucked the pages back into the folder and slid it across the table toward Shay. He stood and opened the door to leave but paused and looked back at her. "Listen, all relationships are complicated, but once a restraining order is involved it's safe to say it's over. This order is temporary and will expire in three months. As long as you leave Mr. Matthews alone, I don't see why he would have any reason to extend it. This will all eventually pass."

Tears of frustration blurred her vision. "What about Roman?" she said, voice cracking. "How do I start an appeal for him?" Her savings account wasn't large, but there had to be enough for a lawyer.

"That's already finalized. The deportation process had already started before he even came in." The Lieutenant rubbed his forehead like he had a headache.

"Go home. And be happy you're not sitting in jail right now." He walked out, leaving the door open behind him.

****

Shay went directly to George's and flew into Raul's office, surprising him at his desk. "Raul, I need Gisella's phone number and any other emergency contact information you have for Roman."

"What happened?" He stood and shut the door.

"I don't know if I can tell you." She didn't want to jeopardize the small chance that Roman still had a job here and the smaller chance he could even get back into the country if he was deported.

Raul looked at her, his face a mask of compassion. "You have my word. I am a vault."

"He's being deported." She felt her face twist with the weight of guilt as she said it out loud. "The police have him and said ICE is coming now."

He took a deep breath and opened a drawer of files, plucking out Roman's. He slid out a piece of paper and handed it to her. She quickly scribbled Gisella's number onto a sticky note and slid the paper back to Raul. "I also have to quit."

"Why? You quitting won't fix things for him with George."

"It's not that. It's a personal reason. I'm sorry." Her words caught in her throat with the realization another thread that made up the fabric of her life had unraveled. *There are other waitressing jobs.* She took a deep breath. "You've been good to me. Thank you."

"Can I do anything?" Raul's eyes searched hers.

"No. This is plenty." She indicated the slip of paper with Gisella's number.

"If you need it, I'll give you a glowing reference." He gave her a warm smile and reached out a hand across his desk that she grabbed and squeezed.

"Thank you." She pulled back.

"Gisella needs to move quickly. Once ICE has him...people aren't always where they should be."

His eyes held a sadness that made her pause. "Take care, Raul."

"You, too."

She couldn't say goodbye to anyone else. That would tip her past her breaking point, and she wasn't done yet. She still had to call Gisella and didn't have a way to do it privately. The anger Roman had exploded with when he destroyed her phone was a sidebar of pain that she hadn't yet addressed. *He believed Kyle.*

She pushed the thought down and strode to the small service station tucked behind the bar. It had a phone she could use out of sight.

Shay hadn't expected Gisella to answer an unknown number but was surprised by her smooth voice after just two rings.

"Hello?"

"Hi, Gisella? This is Roman's friend, Shay. We met last week. I'm sorry to call like this."

Friend. The first pang of deep regret hit her. He hadn't even looked back when they led him away. He thought she was a lying extortionist. Worse, he pretty much ruined his life by trying to help her. They'd never be friends again.

"Shay? Hi, hello, of course. Is everything okay?"

"No." Shay's heart galloped in her chest. *Rip off the bandage.* Raul's warning about time being important rang like an alarm in her mind. "Roman is at the Portland Police Station being held for ICE to deport him."

"What?" Her voice raised. "Impossible."

"I'm so sorry." She couldn't stop apologizing. "I will help any way I can. I have some money for a lawyer—"

Gisella cut her off. "No, they can't deport him. He's not illegal. This is some type of misunderstanding."

"The police told me it was already set up. He was going with ICE. No waiting. No trial."

A string of angry Spanish came over the line before Gisella switched back to English, and Shay heard her telling someone what she'd just relayed.

"Shay, I'm going to put you on the phone with my friend."

She nodded, temporarily forgetting how phone communication worked in the surreal nature of the situation.

A reassuring male voice came through the line. "Shay. My name is Pete Moss. Where is Roman right now?"

"He's at the Portland police station, or at least he was when I left half an hour ago."

"Okay, good. And someone told you the deportation was already arranged?"

"Yes, his name is Lieutenant Bask. But if Roman isn't illegal, I'll go back and tell them that."

"Don't do that, Shay." His voice stayed even. "I'm sure Roman has already mentioned that. Either they'll let him go, or they won't, and if they don't listen to him, they won't listen to you. Was Kyle Matthews involved in this?"

She sucked in a sharp breath. "Yes."

"Shay, it's going to be okay. I promise you, I will get him out. You need to stay away from this. Stay away from the police station. Stay away from Kyle. Do you understand?"

"Yes." She bit her lip. Pete knowing about Kyle meant Roman had already started telling people about the train wreck she had gotten him into. And it was only getting worse.

"Good. Don't worry. Things will be okay. Is this a number I can reach you at?"

"Um, no." She was thrown off balance by the soothing quality his reassurance had on her fragile state. "I have to get a new phone."

"Okay. When you do, call Gisella and let us know how we can reach you." His calm voice reinforced her guilt. She shouldn't even be interacting with these people. There was zero chance Shay was going to reach out to Pete or Gisella again. This was Roman's friend and his girlfriend. She'd brought a tornado to their door, and they still thought they should be kind to her. Gisella could afford a lawyer a million times better than what Shay would be able to offer. And the way Pete spoke belayed an underlying confidence that he wasn't making empty promises when he said he'd help Roman. Shay had no further place here.

"Shay—" Pete's steady voice only made her feel worse for making such a mess for Roman's friends to clean up.

She cut him off. "Thanks. Tell him I'm sorry." Before he could add anything else, she gently hung up the phone. On the other side of the bar Alex chatted up two regulars, and Shay tried to sneak by but caught his eye. He took one look at her, and the easy smile fell off his face. He excused himself and followed her as she rushed outside.

"What happened? Shay, what happened?" He caught up to her on the sidewalk.

"Kyle's trying to have Roman deported, and he got a restraining order against me, and oh, God, I had to quit. It all happened really fast." She was using all her resolve to not shatter.

"What? How? A restraining order against you? He's insane."

"It's all a mess. I don't know. Gisella said Roman's legal, and she's going to fix it. I just want to go home. Can we talk later?"

"Yeah, yes, of course. Call me later."

She nodded, hating how deep the concern ran in his eyes. She didn't remember until she got in her car that she didn't have a phone to call him. The thought was so practical it made her laugh. The laughter quickly turned into muffled sobs as she buried her head in her hands.

One minute. She glanced at the clock on the dashboard. It was a trick she'd learned a long time ago. Give yourself one minute to cry when you really can't hold it any longer, then move on. Otherwise, the sadness could consume you.

Chapter 9

Kyle

This was more fun than he expected.

Across the street from St. George's, Kyle had the perfect view to watch Shay crying in her car. He could have guessed she would come here, but he'd followed her from the police station just in case. Rage coursed through his veins. If that dishwasher hadn't destroyed her phone, this boots-on-the-ground approach wouldn't be necessary in the first place.

Kyle had enjoyed complete access to Shay's phone ever since he'd piggy-backed a nice little malware program onto the pizza meme he sent her. The second she clicked that link he had her passwords, her calendar, her constant whereabouts, and most importantly, the ability to pair her phone with his iPad. That stroke of genius still had him patting himself on the back. He'd sent himself the extortion texts from the iPad which meant they'd also showed up on her phone.

He sighed and forced his shoulders to relax. She'd buy a new phone soon. As long as she used the same account, he'd have instant access. And if not, he'd find a way. Until then, he'd keep tabs on her. Kyle had been sure of one thing since he first saw Shay at a night club a few weeks ago—he couldn't take his eyes off her.

That night, he'd already been watching the front

door of the club for an hour and was thinking about calling it a night when she'd finally walked in. Even if she hadn't been striking in an electric-blue cocktail dress, the scowl on her face would have made her stand out. Kyle ordered another club soda with lime and found a spot one level up where he could lean against the railing and have a clear view of the dance floor and bar below.

A waitress approached Shay's group with a tray of shots, and Shay took two back-to-back, grabbing a third before the waitress walked away. She didn't join in the gleeful cheers of her friends, and the frown was still planted firmly on her face.

What's got you so distressed tonight, beautiful girl?

Her friends pulled her out to the dance floor, and she swayed side to side without making any real attempt at dancing. She did manage to down a couple more shots when trays came by. Kyle's grip on the railing in front of him tightened as a guy approached her. She waved him away, and Kyle smiled. He wasn't good enough for her. That guy didn't know the world Kyle lived in existed. Below, Shay drifted away from her friends and made her way to the bar. *Perfect.* Kyle pushed off the railing and cut a path through the crowd to come up behind her.

The bartender slid her drink toward her, and she turned, almost running into him.

"Sorry." She tried to walk past without giving him a second glance. He sidestepped to cut her off, and she wobbled slightly but caught herself and slurred, "Do you mind?"

"Actually, I do." He raised an eyebrow as he gave

her a half-smile and leaned in. "I was coming here to buy you a drink but since you already have one, I'd be willing to keep you company until you're ready for me to buy your next one."

"No thanks. I've been here for hours. This is my last one."

A spark of anger flicked at her lie, and Kyle ran his tongue across the perfectly even façade of his veneers. "How responsible of you." *Keep it together.* "Look, I'd really like to get to know you somewhere less—"

"No." The group to Shay's left moved away from the bar, and she stepped into the opening their absence provided, then disappeared into the crowd.

Kyle's mouth hung open. A small laugh escaped him. The shock of her dismissal fanned the flame in his chest. But instead of pure anger, it was now edged with excitement. *A chase.*

He cracked his knuckles and took the stairs two at a time to return to his perch. Over the next hour, her drinking slowed considerably, and whatever had been holding her back from dancing didn't hold her back any longer. She moved like she wasn't aware anyone else in the club existed. She was effortlessly beautiful, and Kyle was mesmerized until she broke the trance by making her way back to the bar.

More people had filtered in throughout the night, and it took Kyle twice as long to get down the stairs. By the time he reached the first floor, it was a few minutes before he spotted her in the shadows, leaning against a wall.

She shooed away a guy who reeked of cheap cologne when he passed by Kyle. Kyle shook his head and smiled. Not exactly stiff competition tonight. He walked up to Shay as she drained the last of the bottle of water in her hand.

He'd take a gentler approach. "Hi. You want some company?"

She swayed as she leaned toward him and raised her voice louder than needed to be heard over the music. "Listen, I'm sure you're nice. But even if things went well, you probably have a *Gisella* lurking around ready to pounce."

Man, she was drunk and making no sense, but he could play along. He put an arm around her. "I promise you, the only one ready to pounce around here is me."

"I'm good. Thanks." She shrugged him off and started to walk away.

"Wait." He gritted his teeth. "Please, I just want a chance. Can I get your number?" He didn't usually take the pity route to get a girl's attention, but it worked. She reached into her purse and pulled out a pen, scribbling her number on the back of a receipt.

He took it and promised, "You won't be sorry."

"Oh, I don't doubt that," she slurred and walked away, disappearing into the swarm of bodies on the dance floor.

He was still watching her when she stumbled out of the club and into a cab a few minutes later. He'd mulled over the urge to follow her and take advantage of her drunken state, but no, he wanted more from her.

It was a few days before he called. He figured she'd made him work for it. Now she could sweat a little wondering if he wasn't that interested. When he finally dialed the number she'd given him and found it was fake, his internal scale tipped from infatuated to infuriated. It was an often-overlapping area for him, but he'd never felt such intensity toward someone he wasn't already well invested in. This was new territory, and his anger excited him even more.

He had the receipt she'd written her number on. It was from a local coffee shop at seven-o-two a.m., and he rolled the dice taking a seat there at six thirty the next morning to wait.

By seven ten he started to think it was a waste of time as he added sugar to his refill before leaving. He stood at the counter with the self-service milk and creamer when she walked in. A small victory was in his hands as she made a beeline toward him after she ordered. He gave her a smoldering smile.

Instead of surprise, or even recognition, she gave a polite smile. She stretched one arm to the side of him, plucking napkins from the dispenser, then returned to the coffee bar when the server called her name.

He stood there, floored. She was either playing a crazy game, or she really didn't remember him.

This was a rollercoaster of emotion that he didn't want to get off.

And the ride was only getting started. The buildup leading to the scene at the police station had been incredible. Watching her, being in her apartment, breathing in the scent of her, circling closer and closer. Every time he was sure he'd won she'd change the game. But today, the tables had turned in his favor.

He savored the memory of the crushing blow he'd delivered at the police station as he watched her wipe her face and pull out of her parking spot in front of George's. Now that the glorified busboy was out of the way, he could really have some fun.

He may have been overreacting with the

deportation. If the cook was as interested in Shay as Kyle feared, he would've been at her house last night. Instead, she'd had a sleepover with the gay bartender. His father would be furious if he found out that Kyle had paid off a high-ranking ICE officer to speed up their usual process. He shouldn't have even paid the bribe. He'd basically done their job for them by hacking into their system and finding the dishwasher didn't have an active green card. It had been a risk that came with significant consequences if he got caught. Still, it was worth it knowing Roman Garcia was somewhere in handcuffs on his way back to Colombia.

That left Shay almost alone.

He couldn't make her love him yet, but he could make her cry. It would be interesting to find her exact breaking point. He had the feeling he hadn't even come close. Yet.

But he would.

Chapter 10

Shay

Outside George's, Shay wiped the last of her tears away and went home to come up with a game plan. There was no point looking for a new job in Portland. Anywhere close would risk running into Kyle. Instead, she focused on touristy areas within a half-hour drive and made a list of ones to check out in person. She went to bed with Bear snoring next to her, sure she'd figure out a way to work around the limitations Kyle had set.

The next morning, the first thing she did was buy a new phone. As soon as it finished programming, a voicemail from an unknown number popped up, and a sensation of foreboding settled over her. She pressed play as she climbed into her car.

"Hi. I'm calling from Portland General. Alex Brown was admitted from the ER last night, and you're listed as his emergency contact…"

Shay slammed the gear shift into reverse and floored it out of the parking lot.

It was a miracle that she didn't end up in an ambulance herself after the reckless way she drove to the hospital. The message hadn't said what happened or how he was. No matter what information they would be able to give her over the phone, she needed to see him, and she didn't waste precious time returning the call.

Instead, she made it to the hospital in record time and ran to the reception desk.

The clerk there took her frantic begging for information in stride and calmly asked for Alex's information. After a minute that lasted an eternity, he looked up from the computer at Shay with a smile. "Room 303B. Third floor."

A room number. Thank God.

She took the stairs two at a time, raced through his door moments later, and found him sitting up in bed, eating a pudding cup. She flung herself at him as tears of relief sprung to life in her eyes.

"Hi. Ow," he said, and she loosened her grip. "How did you know I was here?"

"I'm your emergency contact, but I didn't have a phone until right now. What happened?" She stepped back and looked him over not seeing any apparent bruising or injury.

"Some dumbass tried to mug me when I was walking home from work last night. Joke's on him. I've been practicing karate since second grade after Jimmy Watkins pushed me down and called me a name I refuse to repeat. The idiot last night walked away emptyhanded."

A knot unwound from between Shay's shoulder blades. "So why did they admit you?"

Alex rolled his eyes and sighed. "He got in one lucky punch, and I fainted the tiniest bit. My neighbor saw and called 911. Long story short, my spleen is a little dramatic, and the doctors want to watch me for a day or so to make sure it calms down." He opened another pudding cup. "These things are amazing at least."

Shay sat on the edge of his bed and relaxed. "Did they catch the guy?"

"No. But I hope wherever he is, his spleen feels like shit too."

Shay laughed and slid off his bed to take a seat in the bedside chair then froze as her gaze landed on the bouquet on the windowsill. Pink roses. "Who sent those?"

"I don't know. I thought they came with the room."

Shay crossed the room and read the card aloud. "Get well soon, Alex."

"That's so weird. No one knows I'm here. I wonder who else the hospital called?"

A chill went down Shay's spine. "They didn't call anyone else. This was Kyle."

"What? Why do you think that?"

She turned to face him. "He gave me the exact same bouquet the night of our date."

Alex's jaw dropped open. "You're kidding."

"I'm not."

"Shay." He shifted in bed and winced. "That guy really came at me. If I didn't know how to defend myself, I don't know what would have happened."

"Did you see him?"

"No. It was dark, and he came up behind me. It all happened so fast." He shook his head. "We need to go back to the police."

"With what? A hunch and some flowers? He has a restraining order against me. There's no way they're going to listen."

"Well, we have to do something. This guy is dangerous."

"I know he is." She crossed her arms in front of her

chest and fought back tears of frustration. "I've lost my job, Roman is God knows where, and now he's attacked you, all because I ruined a date and embarrassed him. I don't know what to do."

"Come here." Alex opened his arms, and she sank onto the bed next to him. After a moment she pulled back, and Alex rubbed her back. "Listen, I get why you don't want to go to the police, but that means you can't stay here. Do you have anyone you can go visit?"

She bit her thumbnail and shook her head. "No. And even if I did, I don't want to put a target on anyone else's back."

"Then take a vacation. Hell, go live on vacation. You can sell jewelry in Hawaii, right?"

Shay laughed, but an idea started to take shape, and a blossom of hope surged inside her. "It's not a terrible idea."

"Please. It's a great idea. And the restraining order ends when?"

"In three months."

"Perfect. Take three months at the beach and if he leaves you alone once the thing expires, you'll know he moved on."

It was a great idea. "I'm going to do it. But I don't need a vacation. I need a fresh start. There's nothing here for me anymore. School's done. I have no job…" *No Roman.*

Alex cleared his throat, and she smirked at him. "Don't give me that. You told me you were thinking about taking a job on a cruise ship. You're not permanent here, either." She grabbed his hand. "But you'll have to come visit when I settle somewhere."

"Obviously." He rolled his eyes and squeezed her

hand. "Don't write or call."

She laughed, trying not to cry. "I'll let you know I'm okay once I've settled somewhere."

When she walked out of the hospital a few minutes later, she began to make a mental list of what needed to be done. She'd leave this week. Her lease was month-to-month so the most she'd lose there was a few weeks rent. There was a nice cushion in her business account that would be more than enough to give her time to get on her feet somewhere.

Her mind was still turning over logistics when she approached her car. Head down, she didn't see the note tucked under her windshield until she was about to open her door. Tentatively, she reached out and unfolded the paper.

Miss me?

"So, do you?" Kyle's voice right behind her sent a shockwave of fear through her, turning her blood to ice.

She dropped the note and hoped her voice sounded more angry than afraid. "I'm not violating the restraining order if you're stalking me."

"Relax. I'm not here to get you in trouble." He leaned his side against the hood of her car and crossed one leg over the other. "I figured now would be a good time to talk, since you've probably realized the scope of things." He glanced toward the hospital. "How's your friend in there?"

He's been following me. Thinking fast, Shay willed all the anger, frustration, and fear to surface. "I don't know. He's refusing to see me." She glared at Kyle. "It seems he thinks the attack last night is somehow my fault."

"He's not wrong. Although, I only meant to send a

message, not land him in the hospital. Kid can fight." Kyle rubbed the dark shadow of a bruise on his jaw.

"Consider your message received. I've lost my friends and my job. Feel free to leave me alone now." She pulled open her car door and slid into the driver's seat, hoping her message got across. *I have nothing left.*

"If only I could." He pushed himself off the hood and grabbed the top of her door, preventing her from closing it.

"My life is completely fucked up. What else could you possibly want, Kyle?"

"The same thing I've wanted all along. I can't seem to get you out of my head. I think we got off on the wrong foot, and I'd like you to give me a second chance."

Shay was stunned into silence. "You can't be serious."

"I'll drop the restraining order."

"I can live with a restraining order that keeps me away from you."

"If any new job does a background check it won't look good." He licked his lips. "And I could always change my mind about pressing charges."

The realization that he wasn't going to give up settled in her stomach like lead. *Play dead.*

She sank back into her seat and looked up at him, making a point to raise her eyebrows. "You'll cancel the restraining order?"

"It'll be taken care of by the end of our date tonight."

Her stomach turned at the thought, but she needed to keep the illusion going. "And Roman?"

"The dishwasher is out of my hands. Sorry." The

apology didn't reach his eyes.

She swallowed the bubble of helpless rage that started to surface. "And if the date goes nowhere?"

"If I can't win you over, I'll leave you alone. But trust me, I can show you a life you've only dreamt about."

Shay fought the urge to cringe. "Okay."

A wide grin spread across his face. "I'll pick you up at seven." He stepped back, smiling with satisfaction and tapped his fist on the hood of her car.

She plastered on a smile and didn't let the corners of her mouth drop until they were on the highway. His Lexus shot ahead of her, weaving in and out of traffic before it disappeared in the distance.

****

The rest of the morning passed in a whirlwind of packing and phone calls. Her landlord jumped at Shay's offer to leave her furniture so the apartment could be listed as fully furnished. Her donation got her out of the fee that would normally come from not giving a thirty-day notice. It also came with the bonus of having the apartment still look lived in. Hopefully, Kyle wouldn't realize she'd left for good.

She loaded her car, scanning the street for any sign of a car too expensive to fit in her neighborhood. On her way out of town a few hours later, Shay stopped at her cell phone providers' store to change her number then crossed the street to her bank and closed her account. If she was going to run, she'd cover her tracks as best she could. Cash only from here on.

As her car pulled onto the highway, an unexpected feeling of freedom washed over her. The weight that came with being watched fell away with every mile she put between herself and Kyle. There was a six-hour drive ahead of her to shake it off completely. She'd chosen to fade into the background in Lake Placid, NY. The Olympic training center there brought a year-round revolving door of people to the area. That meant there were a lot of restaurants to find work and multiple short-term housing options.

She only stopped once for gas and to check her phone. It was habit. There was nothing to see, and there wouldn't be. She'd reset it to factory defaults right after changing her number and had deleted all her social media accounts. No one had any way to contact her. There wasn't much risk of someone trying besides Kyle. Alex knew better, and she doubted Roman would ever want to speak to her again.

The memory of him being handcuffed while refusing to look at her cut like a dull blade. It added to the layers of guilt she already felt, but she couldn't blame him. Helping her had gotten him fired, then deported.

She turned her attention to the road and flipped on her headlights as the thick canopy of trees overhead filtered out the approaching twilight. Soon, she'd be there and find a roadside motel to stay the night.

Tomorrow, her new life would start, far from Kyle Matthews.

Chapter 11

Kyle

Kyle stood on Shay's front porch at seven p.m. sharp, holding a bouquet of two dozen pink roses. "Fucking bitch," he mumbled and knocked on the door a second time. He'd given up on ringing the bell but refused to believe she wasn't home, despite her car being gone. He pulled out his phone and called her, only to find her number disconnected.

"Fucking bitch!" He slammed the bouquet into the side of the railing, sending petals raining onto the floorboards. He glanced at the empty spot in her driveway again then turned and hit the bouquet into the railing over and over again until the porch was littered with petals.

He dropped the ruined flowers and clenched his fists trying to compose himself. If she wasn't home now, he doubted she was coming home tonight. The scale inside him tipped firmly from anger into rage.

He strode to his car, flung open the trunk, and yanked out the bag that held his laptop. He stopped himself short of throwing it. Instead, he tugged the driver's side door open and slunk onto the leather seat. He jerked the computer out of the bag and flipped it open.

"You're not here. Let's find out where you are," he

muttered as it loaded up. If he couldn't find a trace of her, he would beat it out of the bartender. The surprise of him fighting back was the only thing that kept Kyle from doing more damage during the fake robbery. This time he wouldn't hold back.

A burst of excitement struck through his anger. He'd put a lot of effort into Shay. Much more than he usually expended. And he'd chosen wisely. She'd proven herself to be more worthy of his attention with each twist and turn she threw at him.

His home screen loaded, and his fingers flew across the keyboard. If the dishwasher hadn't destroyed her phone, he'd still have instant access to her location, and this would be too easy.

Kyle couldn't bring himself to be too mad about the loss. It was more than worth it to see how pissed Roman had been at Shay. The force he put into stomping on that phone left no doubt that he placed the blame for his current situation right where Kyle wanted him to—on Shay.

He may not have full access to her phone anymore, but he still had her passwords. Kyle's fingers flew across the keys as he logged into her bank account. He stared at the screen and ran a hand over his mouth. She'd emptied her account this morning. His bad mood began to fade. She really was running.

But he'd find her. She had no idea who she was up against.

With the money Kyle's family had donated to Harvard over the years, his attending class was more of a formality. There was a degree with his name on it waiting, no matter what happened. His family's name and money may have bought his degree, but he didn't need the help. He had a borderline genius IQ and perfect scores on every standardized test that was ever set in front of him. He maintained a 4.0 GPA while dual majoring in IT and computer programming and still had plenty of free time to explore the darker elements of the cyberworld.

As a kid, being gifted was initially credited for his misbehavior, chalking it up to him being bored when he'd get into trouble at school. That was until he put a pipe bomb in his fifth-grade teacher's tailpipe a few days after she'd belittled Kyle in front of the class. It was annoying that he'd gotten the proportions wrong. The car burned, but she didn't. He smiled to himself at the memory. *Practice makes perfect.*

He spent a few more minutes setting up traps on her email and the lone, rarely used credit card she seemed to have for emergencies only. He'd get an alert if she logged in to either account or used the card. Unless she was sleeping in her car, she'd have to give some form of plastic to book a hotel room. The last thing he did was hack into the E-zPass system and look her up. She'd passed through a toll in upstate New York less than an hour ago. *Where are you flying off to, little bird?*

His heart raced with the small success. She was going to make this fun. He flipped the laptop shut and tossed it on the seat next to him.

The Lexus' engine revved as he shot forward out of the parking space with his heart racing. Once he got home, he'd figure out the best way to get full access to her new phone. He would let her enjoy the illusion of freedom for a good long while. It would make it even better when she realized she was still in a cage.

He'd spent countless hours over the past month gathering every detail he could about her life through the lens of his computer screen. When she didn't recognize him in the coffee shop, he realized it was a second chance to bend the situation in his favor. Suggesting brunch at St. George's for his father's monthly family photo-op set up the re-do with Shay for the bungled night in the club where he failed to impress her.

Through the whole meal, he watched her flit from table to table and in and out of the kitchen, always with a soft smile in place. At one point, the Colombian chef came out and whispered something to her. Jealousy crackled in the pit of his stomach as he watched her face transform when she laughed. Her look of amusement stayed after he returned to the kitchen, and Kyle wished he was close enough to hear what was said, so he could say it to her, too.

He'd pulled up the restaurant's website on his phone while his father ate and his mother drank. The guy who'd made Shay light up was the sous chef, Roman Garcia. Nothing special, and not even an American. Kyle clicked on his headshot and read the short bio where he credited his Colombian heritage for his passion for cooking.

When he glanced up from his phone, Shay was looking in his direction. He flashed another hundred-watt smile, but her gaze flicked right past him, not even slowing as she scanned the room.

"Unfuckingbelievable." It was unsettling not to be noticed when he wanted to be.

When he finally cornered her and asked her out, it went exactly as he imagined it would, right up until she turned him down. He had the sudden, almost uncontrollable urge to grab her by the throat. A cold sweat broke out at the intensity, and he stomped down the reckless desire. He wouldn't do anything to her that he couldn't recover from until he was sure that was his last option. Even if it came to that, he'd be careful to not do it publicly.

The cook turned out to be a bigger problem than Kyle had originally anticipated, but he wasn't a problem anymore. Even though the deportation fell through. It was a simple mistake. The dishwasher shared both a birthday and first, middle, and last name of someone who was here illegally. But it looked like the idiot wasn't even going to sue for illegal detainment, so the whole thing was in the process of being glossed over without any real blow-back on Kyle.

The fact that Roman had already been flown down to a detainment facility in Texas was at least a consolation prize. Shay wouldn't have had the opportunity to explain things to him before she took off. It didn't matter even if she could. Roman's reaction when he read the texts was priceless. Deported or not, he may as well be on another planet for all he'd want to do with Shay.

With the bartender hurt and also blaming Shay, it left her alone. The harder she fought, the more Kyle would enjoy it. Her little disappearing act was just an appetizer.

Chapter 12

Shay

Five months in Lake Placid hadn't exactly been a vacation, but it had been nice to settle into a life where Shay wasn't constantly looking over her shoulder.

Getting a waitressing job was easy, and she found an apartment willing to let her pay cash and go month to month as long as she stayed three months ahead in rent. Once she had her feet under her, she found a workshop and began to build up her inventory. For now, she was still hesitant to call any attention to herself, but she'd put almost enough time and distance between them to feel confident Kyle had left her alone.

She was already less paranoid than when she first arrived. Back then she'd waited four weeks to call Alex, and even then she had used a burner phone.

He'd picked up after just a few rings. "Witness protection."

She laughed. "How'd you know it was me?"

"I didn't. I've answered the same for two telemarketers since you left. How are you?"

"Good. You?" They went back and forth for a few minutes. He'd recovered completely and was eyeing the cruise ship job more seriously with fall approaching degree by degree. She told him where she'd settled, and he reassured her that he hadn't heard or seen Kyle since she left.

Her voice faltered as she asked, "Have you seen Roman?"

"Only for a minute. He came in to get his last check."

Shay exhaled a deep breath. He'd made it back. "They didn't give him his job back?"

"No. Raul said he didn't ask for it. He did ask where you were."

Her heart leapt. "Really?"

"Yeah. I told him the truth. That I didn't know, but I didn't think you were coming back soon."

"What did he say?"

Alex hesitated. "He said, 'good.' "

She swallowed the lump in her throat and closed her eyes. "Did he say anything else?"

"Not really."

"Not really, or no?" With no answer from Alex, she probed, "Come on, Alex."

"Fine. I asked him if I should let him know if I hear from you. He said no."

"That's it? Just, 'no'?"

"His exact words were, 'Please, don't.' I'm sorry, Shay. He's really pissed."

"I know. It's okay." Needles of oncoming tears stung the back of her eyes. "Thanks, Alex. I'll call you again soon."

"Okay. Take care. I miss your face."

"I miss you, too."

Any lingering thought of going back to Portland, or even to another part of Maine, faded to a deep corner of her mind after that conversation. And even though it was only a few months later, it felt like years had passed.

Shay stepped through the front door of her small apartment, and her phone pinged with a new email alert. She sat down at her kitchen table and swiped open the email.

It was an invitation from Alex to his going away party at George's that weekend. When they'd last spoke over a month ago, he'd said he was close to sure he was taking the cruise job. He must have taken the plunge. She was about to delete it but hesitated.

It would be so good to see him. And she did have to go back eventually. In her rush to leave, she'd forgotten to clear out her safety deposit box. It had her passport, along with other documents important enough that they couldn't be abandoned forever.

Alex had assured her over and over that Kyle never bothered him or approached him in any way. Plus, he'd never bothered reinstating the restraining order when it expired two months ago. She'd waited long enough.

She smiled as she opened a browser window and booked a hotel. As the transaction processed, she pulled out her phone and sent a text to Alex.

—Got your invite. Just booked a hotel. It will be soooo good to see you.—

For the first time in five months, she felt a hint of being free. She sighed, and her phone pinged with an incoming text from Alex.

—I can't wait.—

****

Friday came up fast. Before she knew it, she was stretching kinks out of her neck from the six-hour drive while waiting in line to check into the Portland Royal hotel.

"Good evening. Welcome to The Royal."

"Hi, I have a reservation under Jane Smith." She felt free, not reckless.

"Yep, I have you right here. Enjoy your stay, Ms. Smith." The receptionist wrote her room number on the key card's envelope and slid it across the desk.

Shay took the key and hurried to the elevator. Thanks to traffic, she was cutting it close, having only an hour to check in and get ready. She threw her overnight bag on the bed and pulled out her makeup and toiletries to take to the bathroom. A quick shower washed the drive off.

Feeling refreshed ten minutes later, she toweled her hair as she stepped out of the bathroom. She froze in place, staring at the bed. Right between the pillows lay one pale pink rose. Swallowing a lump in her throat, she raced to the door and found it still locked.

Her heart pounded as she scanned the room, but she saw nothing out of place. Shay dropped to her hands and knees to look under the bed. Nothing. She rushed to the closet and flung open the door. No one. As the adrenaline rush faded, she scolded herself. She must not have noticed it earlier. It was exactly the nice sort of touch the hotel probably had in every room. Shaking off the uneasy feeling, she finished getting ready and rushed out the door. On the elevator ride down, she took a moment to check that the pocketknife she'd brought at the last minute was in her purse. That small bit of security eased the last of her worry by the time the doors opened.

As she approached George's, a car pulled out of a spot right in front of the restaurant. Taking it kept her from being more than a few minutes late. She stepped into the reception area, carrying a gift bag that held a bottle of the Anejo Tequila that Alex loved.

An unfamiliar hostess smiled at her. "Good evening. Do you have a reservation?"

"Hi. I'm here for Alex's party."

The hostess glanced down at the reservation book. "Do you have a last name for the party?"

"Alex Brown. He works here." The hostess still seemed to draw a blank, and Shay added, "The bartender. It's his going away party."

"Alex Brown?" She looked even more puzzled. "His party was last week. He left for Florida on Monday."

A lead pit of dread formed in Shay's stomach. "My mistake. Thanks." She turned quickly, in a rush to get back in her car and get the fuck out of Portland.

She stepped on the sidewalk, and her heart dropped to her stomach. Across the street, her car was being pulled onto the bed of a tow truck. Panic grew as she ran to the man operating the lift.

"Hey, excuse me. I paid for parking—the receipt's on the dashboard."

"That's nice, lady, but this car's been reported stolen." The man continued to watch her car inch its way onto the bed of his truck.

"That's impossible. It's my car."

"Then it seems like that will be an easy thing to clear up at the police station." He put the control box back in its cradle once the car came to rest.

"Come on. Look, I have cash," she said in desperation.

"Not interested in being an accessory to a felony." He hoisted himself up into the driver's seat and honked for her to move.

She had no choice but to step back onto the sidewalk and watch him leave. Shay immediately flicked open her rideshare app, which luckily had a car just minutes away. After getting in, she perched on the edge of the back seat. Her foot tapped with nervous energy, and gears turned in her head while she rode toward the police station. Too many things were going wrong to be a coincidence.

She leaned forward. "Excuse me. Can we stop at The Royal?"

It took her minutes to run up to her room, jam everything into her bag, then drop the key at the front desk. She was so stupid for haphazardly risking the life she'd begun to build. The sense of urgency only escalated when they finally arrived at the police station, and she took the front steps two at a time.

Inside, she was crawling out of her skin with anxiety by the time she reached the front counter.

"How can I help you?" a female officer asked in a flat voice.

"Hi. My car was just towed because it was reported stolen, but I didn't file that report." Her words tumbled out on top of each other.

"Okay, take it easy. Your car's been stolen?"

"No. It was reported stolen, but not by me. I shouldn't even be here."

"Well, you are here, so slow down." The officer's voice took on a disinterested tone.

"I think a false report was called in to mess with me."

"By whom?" She looked up to meet Shay's gaze.

"A guy who's been harassing me, Kyle Matthews."

A man in a suit behind the policewoman turned

around at the mention of Kyle's name and looked at her.

"Lieutenant Bask." Shay recognized him even though he'd put on a few more pounds since she last saw him.

"I remember you." He stepped up to the desk.

"I think Kyle may have reported my car stolen. I need it back so I can leave."

"Doesn't he have a restraining order against you?"

"It expired."

"Look up her plates." He nodded toward the seated officer, who typed as Shay recited her license plate number.

She clicked through a few screens. "I see what happened. Her number's one off from a car that was reported stolen. Someone probably entered it wrong."

"So my car was towed because of a typo?"

"Looks that way. Should be no trouble getting it back." Lieutenant Bask turned to walk away.

Shay almost laughed with relief. A stupid mistake was responsible, not Kyle. She needed to look at the invitation again She probably just mixed up the dates.

The officer ripped off a slip of paper and handed it to Shay. "Take this ticket to the impound lot at 312 Water Street. They open at eight Monday morning."

"Monday?" Shay repeated, the apprehension returning like freight train. Her heart hammered and she leaned forward, raising her voice. "He did this on purpose, so I'd be stuck here."

Lieutenant Bask let out a long breath and turned to face her. "Kyle Matthews did?"

"Yes. He tricked me into being here and has been messing with me ever since." Exasperated, Shay caught the look of disbelief that passed between Bask and the officer. Desperately she added, "I'm telling you, he planned this. He was in my hotel room tonight. I'm sure of it now.""

Bask glanced to where a few nearby officers had directed their attention to the scene unfolding at the front desk. "Listen, if you want to wait here, I'll have an officer drive you back to your hotel as soon as someone's free, but you need to stop. If this is some ploy to get Mr. Matthews's attention, I'll have that restraining order back in place before you can make one more accusation."

She bit her lip, frustration mounting. "I want nothing to do with him."

"Good, because from what I remember the feeling is mutual." He turned to a passing officer. "Smith, can you put Ms. Cole in a room until we can get someone to drive her to her hotel?"

"That's not necessary." Shay shook her head. She didn't want to spend one minute more in the police station, and there was no way in hell she was staying in Portland for the night.

She kept her head down and walked away from the front desk. Forget a hotel. She could go to the train station and cut her losses with the car. She pulled out her phone to look up schedules and found she'd already missed the last one going anywhere near Lake Placid for the night.

A man leaning against the wall pitched forward and pulled open the door for her. He tucked a slip of paper into his shirt pocket and mumbled, "I'll drive you."

She glanced up, about to tell him "no thanks" but

stopped in her tracks as familiar blue eyes pierced hers. "Roman."

His face stayed a mask of stone, and he looked away. "There's a hotel on my way to the highway. I can drop you off there." He walked out the door into the night, leaving her hurrying to catch up.

He opened the passenger door of a black pickup truck parked in front of the police station and walked around to the driver's side without even looking to see if she followed.

By the time she climbed in with her bag, he'd already started the engine. And as soon as she shut her door, the truck lurched away from the curb.

"Thanks for the ride." That's the best she could come up with through the dreamlike shock of seeing him so unexpectedly.

He stared straight ahead and sped up. "Whatever gets you away from me."

She inhaled sharply. She'd assumed he hated her, but knowing he did made it hard to take a full breath.

"Roman…" She didn't know where to begin and shifted in her seat to face him. He looked so solid and real, leaning back in the driver seat, one hand on the wheel.

He didn't turn to look at her as he cut her off. "You think I'm stupid enough to believe it's a coincidence my wallet goes missing this morning and turns up hours later in Portland? A city I haven't been to in weeks, at a police station that I have nothing but bad memories in, on the same night you just happen to be there? I don't know what kind of fucking games you and Kyle are into, but I want it clear that I'm not interested in playing."

"I didn't have any part in this! The last thing I want is to cause you any more problems. I'm so sorry." Her voice cracked on the words, and her lungs constricted, desperate for air that wasn't coming. From what Alex had told her, Roman had remained in Maine, moving farther north and opening a wildly successful restaurant. She never thought she would run into him on this trip in a million years.

"Save it. I don't want to hear more bullshit from you." They drove the next ten minutes in silence. She couldn't stop herself from glancing sideways at him, but his face stayed a mask of concentration, jaw clenched, eyes focused on the road.

She sunk into her seat. She should have known the invitation was fake. None of this would have happened if she hadn't opened that email…a chill ran up Shay's spine. The email was sent to her business account, an account she'd only set up last month. If Kyle had found that account, then he'd found her. She had nowhere to go home to.

The vise around her chest tightened as they pulled into the parking lot at the Hampstead Motor Lodge. This would be the last time she saw Roman.

The truck came to an abrupt stop, and he hit the unlock button for the doors.

Her voice shook as she started to apologize one more time. "Roman, I want you to know—"

"Save it. Just stay the hell out of my life."

Her face crumpled, and she hopped down from the truck with her bag.

His cleared his throat. "Hey, you dropped this."

Unable to look him in the face, she glanced at his hand and the folded-up paper he held out. She automatically reached for it.

When she grabbed it, he pressed it into her hand, clasping his fingers around hers and squeezing. Her head shot up. His eyes were pools of desperation and pain, but his words cut through her. "I hope you disappear again." He yanked his hand away.

She shut the door and stepped back, fighting the urge to beg him not to go.

He rolled down the passenger window. "You pull anything else like this, and you'll have a brand-new restraining order."

"I didn't—" she said futilely, but he was already speeding away.

Shay swallowed and glanced at the folded note in her hand.

Open this in your room.

A flicker of hope shot to life in her chest. She took a deep breath of the night's warm air and went inside to check in.

Chapter 13

Kyle

Kyle used one hand to stifle his laugh as he watched Roman peel out of the parking lot at the Hampstead.

A couple of weeks ago, he'd reinstalled the malware back on Shay's phone after she opened an email he'd made look like her EzPass statement. He'd taken his time to upgrade the program which gave him access to her microphone. It was intoxicating to be able to listen in on her life at the push of a button, but nothing had been as satisfying as hearing the whole conversation in Roman's truck as it happened.

Today, he'd listened to every interaction Shay'd had since she'd arrived in Portland. It had all played out so perfectly. He'd swiped a maid's key and gotten in and out of her hotel room, gifting her the flower as she showered mere feet away. The tow truck driver had taken his cash incentive to wait down the block when Shay pulled up. Kyle had even thought far enough ahead to bribe a cop to stall Roman from reclaiming his wallet until Shay arrived. But it wasn't necessary—the timing had been perfect even without that.

Kyle had expected a scene at the police station. But being privy to Roman's unrestrained anger as he drove Shay to the hotel was even better. Roman had demonstrated a volatility when he smashed Shay's phone. The aim of the surprise encounter at the police station was to trigger the same type of outburst, possibly ending in Roman's arrest if Kyle was lucky. Instead, he offered her a ride. It was an unexpected turn of events that put Kyle on edge at first, until he realized that Roman used the opportunity to lash out at her. He could almost respect that.

Kyle relaxed into the leather seat of his Lexus, savoring the victory of the night as Shay made her way into the Hampstead. She was probably close to realizing, if she hadn't already, that all her careful planning and hiding for the last few months were for nothing. He could've had her any time he wanted.

Through his car's stereo, he listened as she checked in. It was tempting to abandon his plan and flush her out tonight. Something simple like a fire alarm, or maybe a real fire. He turned the idea over in his head for a moment, but no. He was getting cocky. No point going off-script. This had been a long time coming, and he wanted to give her space to anticipate his next move. He would stay with his timeline and grab her tomorrow afternoon.

His heart raced at the thought, and he shifted the car into drive before he changed his mind.

He pulled out of the hotel's parking lot, listening to her soft sniffling as she made her way to her room. Her key clicked in the door lock, then it was just muffled shuffling. A few minutes later, she picked up the room phone and called the front desk.

"Hi, I just checked in to room 212, and I was wondering if you have an iPhone charger I could borrow? I just realized I forgot mine, and my phone's on one percent. Okay, great. No, I don't need it tonight. Tomorrow morning is fine. Thanks. Good night." The sound of running water indicated she'd turned on the shower.

The image of her shedding her clothes and stepping into the tub was all the more vivid with the sound of running water filling his car. He could almost smell her favorite lavender shampoo. The line went dead, and Kyle took a deep breath. If her battery had lasted a little longer for the fantasy in his mind to play out, he'd have turned around.

He'd been tapping into her phone for hours now, and the thought never crossed his mind that it could drain the battery. It didn't matter. They should both get some rest. He'd planned long and hard for tomorrow. She would learn to never say no to him again. Kyle sped toward his townhouse, his nerves buzzing with anticipation.

Tomorrow's going to be a big day.

Chapter 14

Shay

Shay's hand shook as she turned off the shower. Her heart hadn't stopped pounding since she powered down her phone moments before. She crossed the bedroom and picked up the note Roman had pressed into her hand. The writing was rushed, but clear and to the point.

Kyle is listening to you through your phone. Pretend to call the front desk looking for a phone charger then wait a few minutes and turn it off. I'll be behind the steakhouse across the street. Bring your stuff, but don't turn your phone back on.

She did as the note directed and slid her room key into the early check-out box on her way out. When she arrived at the steakhouse, she told the hostess she was going to the bar but walked straight past. At the back door, she paused, the note still clutched in her hand. It didn't seem possible Roman could be waiting on the other side.

She took a deep breath and pushed through to the parking lot. His truck was there, like he said it would be. The passenger side lock disengaged as she approached, startling her in the silence of the night. She opened the door and pulled herself in, her heart pounding as her gaze landed on him.

Roman exhaled, his blue eyes shining and the ghost of a smile appearing on his face. Shay opened her mouth to ask what was going on, but his smile faded, and he pressed a finger to his lips. He faced forward and shifted the truck into drive.

Her breathing slowed as they drove, but her heart didn't stop racing. Even when the city fell away and the view out the window became dark woods, the uncertainty of her situation coursed through her veins. They drove for the better part of an hour after exiting the highway, going farther from civilization with each mile.

Finally, the road dead-ended at a parking lot that was mostly full, despite there being no discernible destination nearby. He pulled into an empty space and turned off the ignition. Shay turned to him, but he shook his head. He reached over to take her bag and gestured for her to follow him out of the truck.

They meandered between the unoccupied cars and left the brightly lit parking lot to follow a dark path through the woods. Shay glanced up at the extinguished lampposts overhead. *Where are we?*

Gently lapping water broke the silence as they walked. The path opened to a pier with a sole light at its end, illuminating a sleek ferry. Roman took them halfway down the dock where a small tender was tied. He hopped down into the boat and held out a hand to steady her as she came aboard. Shay perched on the bench seat and turned her head to stare into the night. Across the lake, only more darkness awaited them.

Roman threw off the lines and started the engine, expertly steering them into deeper water. She wrapped her arms around herself against the wind as they sped across the calm surface. Minutes later they approached what Shay mistook to be the opposite shore. As Roman turned the boat in a wide arc, he circled around what turned out to be a large island. A single light shone through the dark, and he pointed them directly toward it. It was another empty dock, and they pulled in next to a carbon copy of the ferry on the other shore.

He pulled her up onto the dock. Her legs were shaky beneath her as they walked to a row of rugged golf carts. They got into the first one, its headlights flickering to life when Roman started the engine. He drove them past a boathouse to a paved trail that wound gently uphill through the woods. For the hundredth time since leaving the hotel, Shay wondered where he was taking her. She was baffled by what could be this far out that would require ferries as large as the ones behind them.

Nothing could have prepared her for when they finally broke through the dense forest. A vast lawn blanketed the wide-open space. The narrow path they traveled was now lit with small lamps running along each side as it snaked its way across the lawn and through overflowing flower gardens.

Ahead of them, their destination rose. The building was made of stone with a soft yellow glow coming from the majority of its five stories of windows. As they came closer, they passed couples and small groups walking in the cool evening air, cocktails in hand. They were dressed up to varying degrees, ranging from cocktail wear to full gowns and tuxedos. Music and laughter filtered out of wide doors that stood open to an expansive porch running the length of the building. Stairs cascaded down to a courtyard, full of more people enjoying the early summer evening. Roman steered them back into the shadows and came to a stop next to an unmarked door with no visible handle.

A camera above swiveled in their direction. Less than a minute later, the door opened to a short but well-built man who stepped back to let them pass. Roman went first, leading them down a dimly lit, narrow hallway. The farther they went, the more he increased his pace. Finally, they entered a starkly plain reception area. One desk with a phone was the only thing there besides bare white walls. The man stepped in and shut the door behind them. All three continued into a second larger room. This one had a wall lined with free-standing metal closets, a few desks, and tables with various computers, machines, and wires.

When the door closed behind them, Shay's ears popped.

Roman crossed the distance between them in two strides and wrapped his arms around her, letting out a huge breath. "I knew it. I knew when they called about my wallet it had to be Kyle. I was going to wait there all night for you to show up," he said into her hair before pulling back and searching her eyes with his. "Are you okay?"

She nodded, not trusting her voice.

He let her go, exhaling loudly as he put both hands on top of his head. "I can't believe you're here."

The other man handed her a paper towel. "Hi. I'm Pete. Sorry. This is all I have."

"Thanks." She took the towel and wiped her damp eyes.

"Let's sit down." Pete took a few bottles of water from a small fridge and put one in front of each of them.

She gratefully drank a long pull from the bottle before asking, "Where are we?"

Roman sank into a chair and leaned forward, elbows on the table. "Welcome to The Sanctuary, a secluded and recently reopened resort. I run the restaurants here, Pete's head of security, and right now you're in the old vault from the hotel's glory days."

"It's my lair." Pete smiled, rolling up his sleeves to show forearms covered with faded tattoos. "We think Kyle's been tracking you. Can I take a look at your things to be sure?" His voice was gentle, and Shay handed over her purse and bag. He took them to a table in the back of the room and put them into a machine that whirred to life with a push of a button.

"A vault?" She looked over Roman's shoulder at Pete as he pulled out her cell phone, powered it on, and plugged it into a laptop.

Roman clasped his hands together in front of his face and stared at Shay like she was an apparition. He cleared his throat and leaned back. "This used to be what people called a grand hotel. It had been empty for years until it reopened a few months back. This room was built to bank standards for holding guests' valuables that they didn't want to keep in their rooms." Roman gestured over his shoulder to where Pete was staring at the computer screen. "When Pete came on, he realized the lead lining meant that electronic signals can't get in or out. We don't advertise it, but we offer some specialized amenities for people looking for Pete's unique skills. Some of that includes scanning guests' electronics, cleaning them up, and adding our comprehensive security system designed by our resident tech genius." He nodded toward Pete.

Pete smirked and glanced up at Shay. "I know, I know. I look too cool to be a computer nerd."

"You get a lot of guests here that are under surveillance?" Shay asked him.

"I wouldn't say a lot, but more than you would think. I've found spouses spying on each other, recording devices planted by paparazzi on celebrities, and all kinds of spyware on people's electronics."

"And you think Kyle is doing that to me?"

Pete said, "We suspected, but..." He looked at the computer screen, leaned back in his chair, and let out a low whistle. "Now we can be sure he was from what I just found on your phone."

"What?" Anxiety blossomed in her chest.

"It's a program running silently in the background. And it's a doozy. It looks like it can access anything you've installed, plus the camera and microphone. And it's been paired to a hidden iPad, which I'm assuming is not yours."

"He's been watching all this time?" A chill ran up Shay's spine.

"Someone has," Pete replied.

"Not someone. Kyle." Roman rubbed his forehead.

"All this time." Every morning over the last few months, Shay woke up worried it would be the day he found her. He'd known where she was all along.

She turned her attention to Roman. "You knew?"

"I was pretty sure. That's why I had to be such a dick in the car. If he was listening—"

"He was." Pete chimed in, then looked up to where Roman was glaring at him. "What? I can see timestamps of when he activated certain features. He had the microphone going right up until the phone shut off."

Shay stayed focused on Roman. "How did you know?" She'd have never suspected anything like this.

"It was the day he had me detained. When I took your phone to look at the texts, I realized that to get to the pizza meme he sent, you had to click a link. It seemed unnecessary considering he could have just sent the image, so I forwarded it to myself to show Pete in case they arrested you and took your phone."

"Kyle thought you were deleting the texts, but you weren't." Shay remembered that day all too well.

Roman nodded. "I knew something was off about it. Once they told me I was being deported, I figured smashing the phone would at least keep him from tracking you until I could get back to you. I didn't want to say anything and give him the chance to cover his tracks. I just never thought you'd be gone when they released me."

"So you never thought I extorted him?"

"Please. I know you, Shay. He could have shown me a video of you typing the words yourself, and I still wouldn't have believed it." Roman surprised her with the ferocity of his statement, and one of the knots that she'd been carrying in the pit of her stomach uncoiled.

Pete jumped in. "Destroying the phone probably slowed him down, but this is not basic hacking. This guy really knows what he's doing. He obviously found another way in once you disappeared. I'll figure it out," he finished confidently and got up to retrieve her bag and purse from the machine in the back. "There's no obvious tracking devices on any of your things, but with your permission, I want to take a closer look and also go through any other electronic devices you have with you."

"I'd really appreciate it. Thank you." The thought that Kyle had been listening to her, possibly for months, made her skin crawl.

"Great. I just need a few details." Pete got a notepad and sat next to her.

Roman excused himself, and Pete began asking questions about her online accounts and passwords, specific dates and times to look at, and anything else she could think of that may be helpful.

"I'll get your stuff back to you as soon as possible," Pete said, closing the notebook when Roman returned.

"Thanks." She didn't know if she even wanted it back—it all felt tainted.

Roman held a folded bathrobe and pair of slippers out to her. "Here, so he can check your clothes, too."

"Could he really have bugged my clothing?"

"I doubt it. Your phone was pretty much all he needed to keep tabs on you, but there's no harm in being thorough." Pete shrugged. "I've found a GPS in a bracelet before, and a microphone pinned behind a button."

If there was a chance Kyle had touched her clothes, she wanted them off her body. So she agreed, and both men stepped out of the room while she changed. When they came back in, Shay handed Pete everything down to her earrings.

"It's nice to finally put a face to your voice, Shay," Pete said as she and Roman were about to leave. She put her finger on the familiarity she felt with him—this was the Pete that Gisella had her talk to about getting

Roman out of ICE custody. His steady voice had been a calm patch in the middle of the storm she'd been in back then.

"Thank you." She didn't know how to put into words the full extent of what she was thanking him for. He'd helped save Roman.

"Come on. I'll show you where your room is." Roman held the door open for her to leave with him.

The hallway Roman led her down took them deeper into the hotel, then up a small flight of stairs ending at a door he opened by typing a code into a keypad. They stepped through, into a subtly beautiful hallway with soft lighting and framed black and white images of the hotel and grounds.

The silence between them was deafening.

She glanced at the images as they walked side by side. "A grand hotel, huh?"

"Yeah. I'll get you a full tour tomorrow, if you want." They stepped into an elevator, and Roman pushed five, for the top floor. "There will be plenty for you to do while you're stuck here." He smiled at her. "Two pools, hiking trails, biking, horses if you're adventurous. Plus, there are daily scheduled events, crafts, exercise classes, food and wine tastings. If you would've come a little earlier, you would have seen the tradition of the Grand Ball every Friday night that we resurrected from the hotel's glory days."

"If only I'd known, I would have made my dramatic entrance yesterday."

"Well, next time." He grinned, and a shadow of the easy flow between them returned. It was different now, guarded, but it was there.

They stopped at a room, and he pulled out a key

card to open the door.

A tension in Shay's chest released as they stepped into the cozy room. Thick carpet, a massive marble bathroom, small sitting area, and a king-size bed laden with plush pillows bathed in warm lighting. On the bed, a toiletry bag with the hotel name embroidered on it sat on top of a pile of folded clothes. She went over and unfolded the XL sweatshirt that rested on top.

"Sorry," Roman said. "Things happened kind of fast today. It's a spare set I keep here for myself, but we'll get you your stuff back tomorrow. If you're hungry tonight, you can get room service twenty-four hours a day. Dial thirty-seven on the room phone, and the front desk is double zero if you need anything else." His words seemed rushed, and Shay was acutely aware that she'd hijacked his entire night.

"Roman, I don't know what I would have done if you hadn't come back. Thank you for everything."

He edged toward the door, and she fought the urge to ask him to stay.

"Don't worry about it. Get some rest, and we'll talk tomorrow." He hesitated in the doorway before reaching back in to pull the door shut. "Lock it behind me."

She let the bathrobe drop and pulled on the clothes Roman had provided. She rolled the waist of the sweatpants a few times and was swallowed up by the sweatshirt before collapsing on the bed. The clothes smelled just like him—fresh soap and aftershave. She didn't even get under the covers before exhaustion overtook her, and her eyes closed.

Chapter 15

Roman

Sleep wasn't coming for Roman anytime soon. It took every ounce of self-control he possessed to leave Shay in her room alone. All he wanted to do was wrap his arms around her and not let go again. But he'd be out of his mind to do that. She hadn't wanted to date him when there wasn't the complication of a psycho-stalker looming over them. If he had any hope of a chance with her, it would be when this was over.

Instead of returning to her room, he made his way back down to the main floor and into the darkened kitchen of the resort's crown jewel, his restaurant, Sueno. He brewed a pot of coffee and poured two cups to take to the vault. Pete had been down there looking into Kyle since Roman received the call that afternoon that his wallet had been turned in at the Portland police station.

Roman had known immediately something was up. Neither his wallet, nor himself had left the island in weeks, and it had been even longer since he'd gone to Portland. It had to be a setup.

The door to the vault shut behind him, and Roman put a cup of coffee in front of Pete then sat down across the desk. "What did you find?"

"A lot, and none of it good." Pete picked up the

coffee, nodded his thanks, and leaned back in his chair to take a sip. "He's been a busy boy since we checked in on him last week."

There had been a cascade of change stemming from Kyle's arrival in their lives. Pete had dropped everything to help Gisella while she hired an army of lawyers to get Roman out of ICE's custody. Even with Pete's hacking capabilities, it took over twenty-four hours to find the Texas detention center where Roman was being held. Once they found him, it took three more days to process all the paperwork and get him out. During that time, Pete dug hard into Kyle's digital footprint, growing more and more worried about who they were dealing with. Pete had waited to tell Roman the worst news until he got home. That night was still burned into Roman's memory like it was yesterday, instead of five months ago.

****

After being released from the detention center, Roman was taken directly to the airport and put on a flight back to Maine. He was exhausted by the time he stepped out of the town car that had taken him home. The ride had been courtesy of the US government, just like the first-class ticket to Portland International. The ICE officials had seemed pretty relieved he wasn't screaming for a lawyer when they let him go, but the five-star treatment suggested they were worried he might change his mind. All he really wanted was a shower and his own bed. His phone not so surprisingly got lost somewhere on his trip down to Texas, but he'd called Gisella from the airport letting her know he was on his way and talking briefly with Pete. Hopefully, she'd let him go to sleep without a big homecoming ordeal. He turned the key in his apartment door and found both Gisella and Pete waiting for him.

"Thank God!" Gisella flung herself at him, squeezing tightly. "Are you okay?"

"I'm fine, unless you cracked a rib."

She swatted at him as she pulled away, wiping her eyes. "Don't do that to me again."

"Trust me, I don't plan on it." Roman looked across the room to Pete. "Hey, man."

"Hey, we need to talk." Pete's ever-present good humor was noticeably absent when he spoke.

Kyle. In the brief phone conversation at the airport, Pete had reassured him that he was keeping tabs on Kyle and making sure he was nowhere near Shay. Better to get it over with now. If they came up with a plan, at least he'd be able to sleep.

Gisella's eyes flicked from Roman to Pete, then back again. "I'll be upstairs if you need me." She squeezed Roman's arm as she walked by.

Pete led Roman to the kitchen where an open laptop waited on the table.

Roman sat. "Tell me." The look on Pete's face had already warned him this was not going to be good.

Pete took a seat across from him, in front of the laptop. "This guy, Kyle, he seemed squeaky clean at first glance. But when I dug a bit, I found two sealed court cases. One from when he was a minor and another in his early twenties. I couldn't get into the Juvenile record, but I unsealed the adult case and found he'd been accused of rape and battery when he was twenty-two. He was found innocent, and there's been no legal issues since."

"Okay." Roman waited for the other shoe to drop.

"Later, I was perusing his financial records and found chunks between ten and twenty-grand had been given to a variety of women up until Kyle was twenty-two. It struck me as quite the coincidence, so I took a dive into the campus police records when he was at Harvard. Two girls filed complaints against him which were withdrawn around the time payments hit their accounts."

"How many altogether?"

"Payouts? Eleven."

Roman let out a slow breath. Eleven girls he probably assaulted and paid off before one wouldn't take the money. "So, you think the lawsuit at twenty-two must have scared him enough to stop?"

"No. I think he got more selective with his victims or found other ways to blackmail them, like the extortion ploy with Shay." Pete took a deep breath. "It was nagging at me that I couldn't get into his Juvenile record, so I went back to it. What I found was a series of firewalls and enhanced security on top of the ones that were built and maintained by the government."

"They put more security on the kid's records than the adults?"

"Someone did, and it's impenetrable."

"Even for you?"

"For now. I'll get it. But it was a thread I wanted to pull, so I went into Kyle's high school file. He was unenrolled his sophomore year. The notation in his record was that it was for psychological treatment."

"For what?"

"That was my question. When I searched the local news from that summer, I found there was a tragic accident of a girl in the same grade as him. One paper interviewed her distraught boyfriend." Pete pulled up a file and turned his laptop for Roman to see. The article had a picture of a younger Kyle standing over a casket holding a single pink rose.

Pete swung the computer back around. "I got into the coroner's report. The cause of death was an accidental fall off her second-floor balcony which struck me as surprising since a fall from that height rarely results in death. I had to read the whole report to get the full picture. There were a few wounds that the coroner noted as being not consistent with a fall, specifically marks that could suggest an attempt at strangulation. He recommended a full autopsy, but her family refused."

"Wouldn't it be mandatory?'

"Only if there was enough evidence to suggest there was foul play. In this case, there wasn't, and the family argued it was against their religion."

"Who cares? Their daughter may have been *murdered.*"

The look Pete gave Roman chilled him. "She was one of five kids from a low-income family, and all four of her siblings wound up with six-figure trust funds when they graduated high school."

Goosebumps rippled up Roman's arms. "His family paid them off to keep them from digging too deep."

"That's what it seems like." Pete paused as the words sank in. "This isn't just a bored rich kid messing around. Kyle is a monster with endless resources."

"Jesus. I'm bringing Shay here." Roman stood up and picked his car keys up from the counter.

"Roman, wait. She's not at her apartment."

"Where is she?"

Pete winced. "I'm not sure."

Roman froze and turned back to Pete. "What do you mean? You said you'd been talking to her, and she was safe."

Pete took a deep breath. "I spoke with her once. She was supposed to call back when she got a new phone. When I realized how dangerous Kyle was, I went to her apartment, but she was already gone."

"How long has she been missing?" His heart hammered.

"Come back and sit." Pete's voice was as calm as a hostage negotiator.

"How long?" Roman tilted his head up to the ceiling closing his eyes. When there was no answer, he exploded. "How long!"

"No one's seen her since the day after you were detained."

An inhuman gasp tore from Roman, and he buried his head in his hands with one soft word escaping, "No."

"It doesn't mean he got to her."

"Well, I'm sure as fuck going to find out." Fear threatened to turn into panic, but he chose to focus on the competing emotion, rage.

"Hear me out first," Pete requested. "If you still want to kill him, I'll go with you and make sure you don't get caught."

Roman searched Pete's face for traces of humor. Finding none, he set down his keys.

"That's it, man. Teamwork makes the dream work," Pete encouraged as Roman followed him back into the dining room.

Roman sat with elbows on the table, hands clasped together. His whole body shook as both heels bounced up and down with nervous energy. He looked across the table at Pete with a mountain of helplessness weighing down on him.

"I think she disappeared on purpose."

"Okay," Roman said, the shaking slowing down.

"She cleaned out her bank account and disconnected her phone."

Across the table, the shaking stopped.

Pete's voices stayed steady and even. "I called her landlord, and he told me Shay ended her lease early. That would be going a little above and beyond if Kyle were behind it. I think she ran."

"So, we have to find her before he does," Roman said. A new level of anxiety roared to life in his chest.

"My thoughts exactly, but I'll warn you, so far she's done a good job. There's not a trace of her anywhere. I'll keep searching until we find her, but meanwhile, I'm also going to follow Kyle to see if he finds her first. He makes a move, and we will be on top of him." Pete hesitated before making his final point. "If she's done such a good job hiding her tracks that I can't find her, most likely he can't either. I think the best thing you can do is leave him alone and let him think you're moving on."

"Yeah, no. I'll move on after he's unrecognizable," Roman said.

"Roman—" Pete started, but Roman exploded.

"No! Best case he didn't kill her, but she's still not here, is she? He has her terrified enough that she uprooted her life and is out there somewhere alone. She's just gone." His voice cracked on the words.

Pete waited a few moments before he continued. "Roman, it's not just you that you need to think about. He could hurt you by hurting the people around you. He could hurt Gisella. She's about to move to Maine permanently, and you would be putting her on his radar if you keep stirring this up."

The truth in his words tore Roman in half. "Fuck." He slammed his fist on the dining room table. He buried his face in his hands and took a few deep breaths. "You need to promise me we'll stay one step ahead of Kyle."

"You have my word. If he leaves a five-block radius of his house, I'll be on him like a rash."

The last thing Pete said during that conversation is what kept Roman going for the past five months.

"We'll find her."

****

But they hadn't.

Watching Kyle because they couldn't watch Shay had turned into a horrible waiting game. This whole time they'd never caught so much as a hint that Kyle was even looking for her. It took a few weeks for Pete to get into Kyle's home computer, but when he did, he set up every trap and notification system possible. He'd scoured every keystroke Kyle made.

It really seemed that it was out of sight out of mind for Kyle. Then today everything happened like a tornado, with Shay landing back into Roman's world with both feet.

In the vault, Roman set down his coffee cup to give Pete his full attention. "Tell me what you found today."

"Two months ago, Kyle's name popped up in a police investigation. I feel like a jackass for missing it when it happened, but the search engine I usually run looks for him as a defendant or a suspect. Here they listed him as a possible witness."

"Witness to what?"

"A murder of a prostitute. Real brutal, beaten then strangled. The police checked traffic camera footage once the medical examiner determined time of death, and his car was on video at a gas station near the site they found the body. They interviewed him along with the other customers that night to see if anyone saw her."

"And?" Roman asked, through a clenched jaw.

"Like everyone else they interviewed, his statement said he didn't. They had no suspects, and the case died."

"But you think it was Kyle?" Roman guessed.

"I know it was." Pete typed as he talked. "I combed through other local prostitute murder cases and found another from a year and a half ago that had been murdered in the same way, beaten then strangled."

"Like he tried with his high school girlfriend."

"Bingo. But that's not all. I looked at Kyle's travel history over the past few years and searched the cities and timeframes he traveled for similar crimes. So far, I've found one in LA, one in France, and a third in England that could have possibly been him. All prostitutes. All strangled."

"Which no one picked up on since they're all over the place."

"Exactly. That's why the payouts stopped to the college girls. He switched from assaulting coeds to murdering prostitutes." Pete flipped his computer screen toward Roman. "Notice anything?"

The images were awful, but one thing stood out.

They were all blondes until the last image. Bile rose in Roman's throat. "The most recent one looks like Shay."

"Yep. Same age group, similar height and build, and the same long, dark, auburn hair."

"Oh, Jesus." Roman sank back in his seat and took a moment to think. "I want at least two people monitoring the security cameras at all times and an armed guard at the docks meeting every ferry."

"You got it. I've almost got it all put together in a neat little file tied up with a bow, and I'm going to reach out to a guy I know at the FBI. He can get it to the right people fast."

"Good thinking. Thanks."

"Any time, boss."

Roman had every confidence that Pete was doing everything he could, and he left to try to get some rest.

He rode the elevator back up to the fifth floor and slipped a key card into the room that adjoined Shay's. A few hours ago it had seemed like overkill, but now knowing what Pete had just told him, he was glad he let his protective instincts drive and had booked himself the room right next to hers.

It was going to be a challenge being around her and not telling her how he felt. How he thought his heart actually broke when he was released from the detention center and found out she was gone. How hard he searched for her. How a day never went by without him thinking of her.

He'd moved forward, building a career and life that lacked the thing he wanted most. To have her here now was bittersweet. No matter what he wanted, she was off-limits until this was over.

Chapter 16

Shay

The message light on her room phone was lit when Shay woke the next morning. Thankfully, it was the front desk telling her that someone could bring up her bag when she was ready. She'd slept fitfully but was too anxious to go back to bed. As soon as the bag came, she took a long, hot shower, willing the water to rinse away her worries.

Wrapped in a towel, she emptied out the bag and wished she was an over-packer. Since this was supposed to be an overnight trip, she only had one spare change of clothes. Her pulse accelerated. She couldn't go back to her house in Lake Placid for her clothes, or her furniture, or her tools...another life she'd have to leave behind.

Her legs wobbled, and she sank onto the edge of the bed. She wasn't going to be able to continue her jewelry business. He'd look for it. The weight that settled on her chest became heavier the more she thought, and her breathing quickened. She stood and crossed to the windows, desperate for more air.

She flung back the curtains, and her rising panic evaporated. The view was incredible. Fresh, golden light of a new day stretched across rolling hills and a lush green forest as far as she could see. The forest was interrupted only by the lake they'd crossed last night. Below, a vast lawn sprawled out from the hotel. There was a free-form pool, remnants of a bonfire, and a huge courtyard. Flowers were everywhere, in every color imaginable. It seemed too beautiful to be real.

Her breathing returned to normal, and she pulled herself together. Stressing about what she couldn't control wasn't going to help. She needed to move forward. To come up with a plan. She had anonymity for now, but there was no telling how long that would last. She needed to figure out where to go next. First step was coffee and food.

When the elevator opened on the main floor, she stepped into what Roman had called the Great Hall. It was a cavernous room with clusters of oversized furniture running down both sides. Daylight flooded in through floor to ceiling windows, and the impressive front double door leading out to the porch was propped open.

As she crossed the dark hardwood floor, she spotted the entrance to the main restaurant, Sueno, and veered in that direction. Inside, a hostess greeted her, then led her across the half-full room to a table beside a window. The restaurant had a simple elegance with white tablecloths and a gentle flow to the layout that angled toward the kitchen.

That was where it was unique. Instead of being hidden from view, the kitchen was on full display behind glass windows that allowed patrons to watch the chefs like a show. It mesmerized Shay as she sipped her coffee and waited for her food.

When it arrived, her omelet was perfectly cooked with just the right amount of melted cheese in each forkful. She ate every last bite then signed the check to the room. She'd have to add figuring out how to access her bank account to the list of everything else that needed to be sorted out.

Before she could stand, Roman walked into the dining room, his gaze landing on her. He stopped at the waitresses' station to pour himself a cup of coffee then sank into the chair across from her. His clothes were the same ones he'd had on last night, and his face wore an uncharacteristic dark shadow of stubble.

"How are you?" he asked.

"I'm okay. Pretty grateful to be here, instead of the Hampstead."

One corner of his mouth turned up. "We have better pillows at least." His smile faded. "We should talk about a plan."

"I agree." She sat up a little straighter. "I have money. I can't access it now, but as soon as I can, I'll pay for the room and meals."

"What? No. The room is yours at no charge for as long as this takes." He frowned and shook his head. "I meant we should talk about how Kyle goes away, and you get your life back."

It was much more than she expected and took her off guard. "I don't want you pulled into this, Roman. He has a long reach."

"He pulled me in the second he tried to have me deported."

Shay's cheeks flamed with guilt. "I can never apologize enough for that. I know you got released, but—"

"You have nothing to be sorry about. Besides, I guess the computer genius didn't do his homework and realize I've been a citizen since my dad brought me here when I was a child. My lawyer had a field day on ICE, and I spent a few nights in an intake holding cell in Texas. I was out before they put me into the general population in the detention center." His lopsided grin returned. "Now I can say I've done cold, hard time, which only backs up my tough-guy image."

"I'm just so sorry about all of it—the arrest, being fired from George's, whatever mess I'm bringing to you now." She wasn't willing to let him dismiss her guilty conscience so easily.

"None of the blame for any of that belongs to you. I was ready to leave George's, and don't forget, I brought you to my doorstep now."

Roman held his mug out for a refill as a waitress brought a fresh pot of coffee by, then returned his attention to Shay. "Pete's reached out to a friend at the FBI who's going to make sure an investigation is started. He's found more than enough evidence on your phone to have a stalking charge be a no-brainer. Once they look over the stuff Pete sent, we'll have a better idea of our options and a timeline. But I think you should stay here until Kyle's in custody."

"I can't do that. I should go to..." She trailed off and glanced down at the tablecloth, not able to come up with a single option of somewhere safe.

"Shay, Kyle was listening to us last night before you turned your phone off. As far as he knows, I want nothing to do with you. So far, Pete's found no way he could have tracked you here since your phone was off during our ride up. This is probably the last place he'll look for you." He paused, then added, "I can't make you stay, but I want you to."

139

The plea in his deep blue eyes made her catch her breath. She'd been painfully aware the constant flirting and light banter that used to define their relationship had not returned. Probably because he'd gotten over whatever infatuation he'd had when he realized she came with a soul-crushing amount of baggage. But this made her heart quicken with the hope there was something still between them.

"If I stay, I want a tab," she said.

"Fine. But I have an in with the owner, and you'll be getting a sizable discount."

A smile spread across her face, mirroring his. "If I'm staying, I need to figure out how to get a few more changes of clothes."

His phone vibrated on the table. He picked it up and glanced at the screen, absently saying, "That's no problem. Gisella is headed to Portland for the night. You can tell her your sizes, and she'll pick up whatever you need to have it here by tomorrow." He stood, still looking at his phone, unaware of the bomb he had just dropped.

"Gisella's here?" She almost choked on the words.

"Yeah. She oversaw the renovations from afar for years but moved here permanently as soon as we reopened. We live on the other side of the island." He typed something on his phone and hit send, then smiled at her. "I asked the concierge, Manuel, to show you around this morning so you get an idea of what there is to do while you're here. He should be in by now, and I'll have Gisella find you later."

She plastered a smile on her face. "Okay, thanks."

She stayed sitting after he left, letting the shock wear off. So, consistent Gisella had become permanent

Gisella, and this was her investment property. The urge to cry welled up, and Shay pushed it down. She needed to figure out how to appreciate this opportunity, no matter how much it hurt. Roman was doing such an incredible thing for her. She had to be grateful and start focusing on the possibility that she would be able to go back to the life she'd built in Lake Placid.

She stood and made her way to the concierge desk and introduced herself to the short, bald, smiling man who waited there.

"Hello, Ms. Shay. I'm Manuel. Very pleased to meet you." He walked around the desk and clasped his hands together. "Would you like to start your tour inside or outside?"

Inviting sunlight poured in through the giant windows. "I could do with some air."

"As you wish," he said, with a slight bow. They stepped out onto the porch, which stretched the entire length of the hotel. It was peppered with rocking chairs, swings, and oversized Adirondack furniture. Vibrant flowers poured out of window boxes attached to the railing and in overhead hanging planters.

He led her down the stairs, through the courtyard, and began the tour. They passed the fire pit that he explained held a bonfire most nights year-round, walked by the outdoor pool, and slowly followed the path across the lawn with him pointing out specifics as they went.

"It's so beautiful here," Shay said as they walked. "How far does the resort's property go?"

"It's the whole island. Eight miles long and four across." Manuel gestured backward since they'd almost reached the far side of the lawn. "This lawn alone is two acres, but Gisella has utilized almost the entire island."

A butterfly meandered through the air between them, and Shay almost had to laugh. Of course this place was as perfect as Gisella.

"Let's get a ride for a bit." Manuel paused in front of a small booth and asked the worker there to pull out one of the golf carts. He gestured toward the booth while they waited. "There are shuttle huts all over. If you ever want a ride, just look for one, and an attendant will drive you wherever you want to go. There are no full-sized vehicles on the property, aside from two emergency response vans."

Shay looked past the shuttle hut to a two-story log cabin perched next to the river. "What's that?"

"Ahhh, that's Farmstand. One of the three award-winning restaurants on the property. The Pub is casual and on the ground floor of the hotel. And Sueno is our crown jewel." His eyes lit up. "It was recently awarded a Michelin Star."

"That's impressive." George's didn't even have a Michelin star.

"Indeed. Roman is the executive chef of all three, but Farmstand is his baby. It's open Thursday to Sunday only, with no set menu since everything is locally sourced. I've worked with a lot of chefs. Sueno is proof that Roman is one of the best, but Farmstand is what shows he is a true culinary genius."

"Wow. Three restaurants are a lot to keep track of."

"Oh, yes. But Chef Roman is made for it. He and Gisella live and breathe this place. They are the reason each guest's stay here is such an extraordinary experience." The cart pulled up beside them. "Here, hop in." To the driver, Manuel said, "Take us for the full tour, Sean."

The cart shot forward and followed a paved path into the woods. It was over an hour snaking through the maze of paths while making stops at the horse stables, an archery range, a zipline course, and a pristine beach that had a swimming area as well as a vast array of kayaks, paddle boards, and canoes.

On their way back to the main hotel, Manuel pointed out trail markers that indicated the difficulty of the many hiking paths that utilized the varied terrain of the island. The driver left them at the opposite end of the hotel from where they started, and they walked through a walled-in courtyard with outdoor seating for a café.

"This is one of our hidden gems." Manuel raised his eyebrows as he led her to the back wall of the courtyard. A small, hidden opening led down a short flight of steps and ended in a sunken garden.

Shay caught her breath. A labyrinth of brick pathways wound through statues and fountains. The flowerbeds teetered between carefully manicured and totally wild with flowers spilling over their boundaries everywhere. A second set of steps led down to an even lower tier, and ancient looking statues were peppered throughout. It was one of the most beautiful places Shay had ever set foot, and she had to drag herself away to continue the tour.

They entered through the café, and Manuel took her through the ground floor. They passed management offices, a gift shop, a game room complete with a two-lane bowling alley, and a world-class gym with saunas, eucalyptus steam rooms, and heated bamboo flooring.

Up one level, they were back on the main floor which was taken up mostly by the Great Hall and Sueno.

By the time they went back down to The Pub, it was early afternoon, and Shay was starving. Manuel left her after she thanked him profusely for giving her so much of his time.

"It was my pleasure," he said. "Oh, perfect. There's Ms. Gisella."

Any hope Shay had that retirement had dulled Gisella's beauty was dashed. If anything, she was more beautiful than the first time they'd met. In a simple sundress with strappy heeled sandals, Gisella broke out into a huge smile as she made her way toward Shay and enveloped her in a surprisingly forceful hug.

"Shay. It's so nice to see you again. Come, sit. Have lunch with me." Gisella gestured back to where she'd been sitting alone at the bar.

Before Shay could decline, Gisella pulled her across the room and asked the bartender to bring a menu. The thought crossed her mind that she should order a salad, so she wouldn't feel like a pig next to the size-two Gisella, but then Gisella's order arrived. A fully loaded cheeseburger with onion rings.

"Sorry, I'm not going to wait for you. I'm starving." Gisella took a bite of the burger and rolled her eyes in pleasure.

In spite of herself, Shay found she liked Gisella and ordered fish and chips that came highly recommended by both her and the bartender.

After finishing her meal, Gisella pushed away her plate, and the small talk they'd been making about the resort turned more serious. "Roman told me some of what you have been going through, and I'm so sorry.

I've had a few instances of unwanted attention."

Shay thanked her. "I think I stumbled into the mess of someone who is the trifecta of rich, powerful, and psychotic."

"Sounds like a few of my exes," Gisella joked. The light caught the diamond on her engagement ring as she folded her napkin. "Sorry. I don't mean to make light of your situation."

Shay took a sip of water to give her heart a moment to slow down. *Engaged?* Another sip, and she set her glass down on the bar harder than she intended. "Oh, don't be sorry. That was funny. I'm glad you found a good one now." It was annoying that she actually meant it. She couldn't help herself. Gisella was so warm and welcoming. In another world they could have been friends.

"I found the best one." She beamed. "And you have nothing to worry about. Pete and Roman are going to get this taken care of for you, freeing you up for the second best."

Shay laughed. Dating wasn't something she'd even considered in the past few months.

Gisella glanced at her phone. "Oh shoot. I need to run if I'm going to make the next ferry. You're about a size eight for clothes, and a seven-and-a-half shoe?" She stood and grabbed her purse from a hook under the bar.

"Yeah, good guess."

"And they say models have no skills." Gisella winked and breezed out of the restaurant leaving Shay unsure if she should laugh or scream.

Chapter 17

Kyle

It wasn't too concerning that Shay's phone still hadn't been turned on when Kyle woke up. She may have slept in or didn't get the charger right away. A long run and shower later, he walked across his bedroom with towel draped around his neck and turned on his iPad. Still nothing. Impatience flared in his chest, and he yanked the towel from his shoulders then slammed the computer shut.

By noon, irritation prickled under his skin like fire ants. It became more uncomfortable by the minute as he drove to the Hampstead. He needed a few seconds to compose himself before walking in so his nervous energy didn't make him look suspicious.

He pasted on the practiced smile, *his mask*. Inside, he strode across the lobby to the elevator, an extra-large suitcase rolling behind him. He was done playing games. On Shay's floor, he stopped in front of her door, smearing lip balm over the peephole. His other hand pulled a hypodermic needle from his pocket and slipped off the cap. He knocked, ready to muffle his voice and say he was from the front desk.

The door swung open to a balding man in his late fifties. "Yes?"

Careful not to stick himself, he palmed the needle.

Behind the man, a woman sat on the bed with an open guidebook in her hand.

"Sorry, I must have the wrong room."

Kyle backed away and walked a few doors down. Rage bubbled behind his ribcage as he recapped the needle. He went to the front desk. It took every ounce of his self-control to stand in line when what he wanted to do was start slamming people's heads together. When he finally reached the front of the line, he leaned on the counter and gave the girl there the most charming smile he could pull off at the moment.

He glanced at the name tag pinned to a shirt stretched to its limit across her chest. "Hi. I hope you can help me, Valerie."

"Me, too." She sat up a little straighter and leaned forward.

"My girlfriend's here for business. I'm supposed to be meeting her here tomorrow, but I came a day early to surprise her. Could you tell me which room she's in?"

"We're not supposed to." She'd deflated at the mention of a girlfriend.

"I forgot our anniversary last week, and I've been in the doghouse ever since."

She scrunched her mouth to the side as she contemplated.

"It would really help me out," he pleaded.

"Okay, fine." She started clicking keys. "Just because I'm a sucker for love. What's her name?"

"You're the best. Her name's Shay Cole." He'd heard her give her real name at check in last night. A detail that suggested she'd given up trying to hide. She had to be here somewhere.

Valerie bent forward. Dark roots showed under her

bleached blonde hair. "Okay, it looks like she checked into room 212 last night but checked out this morning." She looked up at him sympathetically. "Sorry."

"Are you sure she didn't just change rooms?" he asked, barely able to hear her over the blood pounding in his ears.

She was sure, and no, she didn't see her. Shay must have checked out with one of the other clerks. Bottom line, she was gone.

"You know, if you're interested, I'm off in half an hour and could show you around town." She bit her bottom lip in a gesture Kyle was sure was meant to be sexy, but her nails were as fake as Kyle's smile, and God only knew what she actually looked like under the layers of makeup she wore. A smoldering burn crept from his chest to his stomach at the contrast to Shay's natural look.

"I would love that." He forced a smile. "I'll be out front in the Lexus."

Her eyes lit up. "Do you need to book a room?"

"Nah, I'll get one somewhere else. See you in a half-hour." He left, returning to his car where he flung the empty suitcase into the trunk and slid behind the wheel. Again, he checked if her phone had turned on. Still nothing. He squeezed his phone to keep from smashing it on the dashboard. *Think.*

He flipped open his laptop and spent ten minutes hacking into the Hampstead's CCTV system. He could use the time waiting for Valerie to scan through the morning and find when Shay left. If he could get a glimpse of a license plate, he'd be able to figure out which car service she used.

His frustration threatened to spill over when he

went all the way back to four a.m. and still didn't see her. He rewound farther and watched her check-in last night. His index finger trailed gently across the screen where her auburn hair swung softly past her shoulders. He leaned back and picked up his iPad to see if she had popped back up anywhere. Still nothing. He was debating driving away when the video feed showed her striding out of the hotel with her bag not even ten minutes after she checked in. She dropped her keycard in the overnight check out box as she went by.

His breath caught. That bitch. She'd played him. She must have figured out he was listening to her and planned the little charade with the charger. He tried to organize his thoughts as his breathing came rapidly through flared nostrils.

He caught sight of his bloodshot eyes in the rearview mirror and flipped it away with such force it snapped off, landing on the floor of the passenger's side. She wouldn't go back to Lake Placid, but she would need money at some point. He set up an alert on his phone to notify him if she attempted to access her bank account as a sharp knock sounded on his passenger window.

He clicked the unlock button and twisted to put his laptop in the back seat. Valerie had managed to add another layer of makeup to her caked-on look. God, he hated blondes.

"Wow, I've never been in a Lexus before," she cooed, sliding in. "I can't believe your ex stood you up."

"Me neither." He backed out of the space, pressing the lock button for the doors.

"Oh, no. What happened?" she asked, toeing the

broken mirror at her feet.

"An accident." His teeth clenched together.

She shrugged and rubbed her hands together. "So, I was thinking we could start at this bar I love down by the water called McCoy's. They have the best drinks. Then I can show you around downtown."

He knew the bar, a typical trashy tourist spot with sickly sweet drinks. "I want to show you something first." He pulled out of the parking lot and turned onto the highway.

"Ooooh, okay," she purred. "I'm up for anything."

Good.

He yanked the syringe from his pocket and plunged it into her thigh, stopping halfway. The dose should be enough to knock her out for the hour-long drive to the secluded house he'd rented for Shay.

He gripped the steering wheel and took a deep breath. Shay's head start wouldn't matter. He'd find her. He could afford to play for a couple hours and burn off some of this steam. It would clear his head.

He pressed his foot on the gas, imagining the fear in Valerie's eyes when she woke up and realized why you shouldn't get into cars with strangers. Even if they're driving a Lexus.

Chapter 18

Shay

When Manuel pointed the library out on their tour, Shay had been drawn to the inviting atmosphere and made her way back as soon as she left The Pub.

The library door stood open to the hallway. She entered a room with floor-to-ceiling bookshelves and a few sets of leather couches and chairs. She took a lap to see what types of books were on display. As she made her way around the room, she found a thick oak door tucked in the back corner simply marked "Library" in a dramatic scrawl etched into the wood. She glanced around the otherwise empty room then turned the handle and pushed.

The room beyond had the same towering bookshelves, but it also had a full bar stretching across a bank of large windows that let in the warm afternoon light. Afternoon tea service was set up with a wide array of tea, pastry, and coffee selections. A door on the other side of the bar led to a maze of interconnected rooms, all laden with bookshelves and their own nooks and crannies. After exploring, Shay went back to the bar to make herself a pot of Earl Grey tea and settled in the room overlooking the sunken garden.

After a peaceful afternoon, she returned to her room in time to watch the sunset. She sat on the end of her bed with her knees tucked up under her chin. Gisella was a genius. This place was magical.

Shay made her way to Sueno at nine. At night, the dining room was transformed from elegant to ethereal. Soft candlelight drifted from tealights overhead, suspended from the ceiling on translucent strings. The gentle curves of the restaurant and the all-white décor gave the vague sense that Shay was walking through clouds as she followed the hostess to her table.

She sat at a round booth, facing the kitchen. Roman was directly in her eyeline through the glass and instead of picking up her menu, she watched him move smoothly through the kitchen. He had the same look of concentration that she used to love to study when he was working the line at George's and didn't notice she was looking.

Tonight, he noticed. He glanced up, and her eye caught his. His concentration faded into something softer for a moment. Her heart beat fast, then sank at the sight of the dark circles under his eyes. She lifted her fingers over the top of her menu in a wave and turned her attention to the dinner options.

The waiter came and took her order for a glass of pinot noir that she hoped would help her sleep. There hadn't been many nights of great sleep since meeting Kyle, but last night had been exceptionally bad.

Shay jumped as familiar words broke through her thoughts. "*Mi cielo.*"

Her head snapped up from the menu. Next to her, a line cook, who was most definitely not Roman, stood holding a platter with a bowl balanced on top. She leaned back from the table as he placed it in front of her and explained, "Compliments of the chef," before turning away.

A wide smile spread across Shay's face. It was her old favorite—mushroom bisque with garlic chips.

Her gaze shot to the kitchen and landed on Roman, who now grinned, watching her reaction.

She groaned in satisfaction at the first bite. The combination was exactly as buttery and smooth as she remembered.

After another bite, she picked up the menu. The bisque was listed under appetizers as "*Mi cielo*." It was the perfect name—it was heaven. Fighting back the memory of how his voice used to rumble when he'd call her that, she tried not to wonder what he called Gisella.

The waiter returned, and she ordered the special, Seared Scallops with Truffle Mashed Potatoes. The scent of fresh lemon and dill made her mouth water when the waiter set the plate down. It tasted even better than it smelled with the scallops practically melting in her mouth. She'd have to start writing down the meals she ate to track her debt. No matter how discounted Roman tried to make her stay, she would be sending a check as soon as she could get into her bank account. She refused to take any more advantage of his kindness than she already had. And her jewelry business was doing well enough that she didn't need charity. She cringed thinking about the orders that were going unfilled.

Her train of thought was interrupted as Roman slid into the booth across from her. "How was everything?"

"I didn't think it was possible, but you've gotten even better. Everything was delicious."

"Good." He covered his mouth as he yawned.

"You look tired." A pang of guilt struck her. He wouldn't be losing sleep if she wasn't here.

"Nah, I'm good. As I mentioned, Pete's working with the FBI agent. They're probably going to want to talk to you sometime tomorrow."

"Where?"

"They're setting up a secure video feed to do it remotely for now. I'll let you know as soon as they give me a time. How was the tour with Manuel?"

"Amazing. This place is incredible."

"Good. Treat it like you're a guest here, not a hostage, and enjoy yourself." Roman stood to leave. "I'll talk to you tomorrow."

Later that night, Shay pulled Roman's sweatshirt over her own pajamas and snuggled under the covers. It was to keep warm. Not because the scent of him made her feel safe. She took a deep breath and closed her eyes. An image formed in her mind, his blue eyes sparkling with a smile after one of the hundreds of times he proposed to her. Her conscience prickled, reminding her that he was spoken for, and she should take the sweatshirt off.

She fell asleep before she could decide what to do.

Chapter 19

Roman

Roman woke the next morning refreshed, after a more or less full night's sleep compared to the two hours he'd gotten the prior night. Before going to bed, he'd gone to his house and packed a bag so he could stay at the main hotel as long as he needed.

This morning, he put on sweats and headphones and went for a run on his favorite trail that looped through four miles of the hilled property. It usually helped clear his head, but his thoughts still churned when he emerged from the woods, panting, forty minutes later.

After he showered, he found Pete in the Hall talking to the head of one of his security teams, both of them dressed in plain clothes. They had a tech giant staying the next few days, and Pete was going through the routine of making sure the additional security presence wouldn't be noticed by other guests. The VIP's own security team would arrive ahead of him to meet with Pete and get the layout of the property. It was a dance they did often.

Pete caught Roman's eye across the room and excused himself. "Hey, man. You look human again."

"I feel human again." Roman ran a hand over his face. "I'm just glad we're getting things moving."

"That we are. Agent Hiller is good to go at eleven a.m., and I'll have us set up in the conference room."

"Perfect. We'll meet you there."

Pete and Roman separated as Gisella walked in, weighed down with shopping bags from at least eight different stores.

Roman called to her. "Did you leave any clothes at the stores?"

"A girl needs options." She passed, not slowing on her way to the elevator. "And you can afford it."

"I want my credit card back, Gisella," he yelled, which she ignored. "Tell Shay I'll come get her at quarter to eleven for our meeting."

"Will do." She pursed her lips and blew a kiss in his direction.

He went to his office on the ground floor near The Pub to take care of some of the restaurant's paperwork and to try to occupy his mind until the meeting. Shortly after, he found himself pacing the ground floor halls until it was close enough to ten forty-five to go up to Shay's room.

He announced himself as he knocked. She opened the door to a room with clothes and shoes strewn across the bed and furniture. Gisella had chosen well. Shay wore a pair of perfectly fitted jeans with an off the shoulder dark green blouse that brought out the gold in her eyes. The urge to wrap his arms around her came over him, and he shifted his weight to take a step forward.

Stop.

He ran the hand over his short hair instead. She had a psycho stalking her, and he'd pretty much kidnapped her himself. Great start to a relationship. He shook his head. He'd promised himself that he wouldn't so much as flirt with her until this was over and her head cleared from anything Kyle related.

He forced his gaze past her to eye the piles of clothes. A low whistle escaped him as his eyebrows raised.

"I know. It's too much. She's making me nervous that she thinks I'll never leave."

I hope she's right. "She thinks you need choices."

"Well, I've got them." Shay joined him in the hallway and tucked her room key into her back pocket.

In the elevator Roman stared at his shoes. Being this close to her bordered on torture when he couldn't say what he wanted. *Don't leave me.* A stupid, worthless thought. It hadn't worked on his mother, no matter how much he or his dad had wanted it to. One-sided love wasn't enough and if anything, Shay seemed to be more uncomfortable around him every time their paths crossed.

The elevator doors opened, and he led her to a meeting room with what he hoped was a reassuring smile. Pete sat at one end of the table with a laptop in a heavy-duty protective case. On the screen was Agent Hiller. Roman had spoken to him on the phone, but he'd never seen him face-to-face. Hiller fit the image of what Roman pictured an FBI agent would look like—short-cropped black hair, freshly-pressed suit, and ramrod straight posture.

An air of nervousness radiated off Shay once they made their introductions. He inched his chair closer to hers but refrained from reaching out to touch her.

Agent Hiller didn't waste time with formalities. "Hi, Ms. Cole. Tell me from the beginning everything you remember from your relationship with Mr. Matthews."

Her breathing hitched at the word relationship, but she dove in, going over everything from their first meeting to the details of Kyle harassing her when Roman was detained. His fingernails dug into his palms as Shay described what she had gone through.

A burst of fear coursed through him when she detailed her life in Lake Placid. Even if a miracle happened and he could convince her to give him a chance, she wouldn't want to leave that to be with him. He steadied his breathing. *So I'll move.*

Roman sat back in his chair and rolled his eyes, rubbing both hands over his face. He needed to get his head in the game. This was the exact type of distraction that he couldn't have until she was safe. *Focus.* He leaned forward, rested his arms on the table, and gave the present conversation all his attention.

Agent Hiller had Shay go through certain parts of the story repeatedly, and it was exhausting to watch. She kept her composure throughout the interview. If anything, she became more sure-footed as they continued and she remembered new details. She was so much stronger than he'd thought, and he'd already thought she was pretty strong.

Strong and beautiful...

He bit the inside of his cheek hard.

He needed to keep more distance from her.

It should help that she didn't have the same spark for him that she used to, but that just made it worse. Since she arrived, she volleyed between disinterested and apologetic. A combination he hated.

"Thank you, Ms. Cole. I think that's all I needed

from you. I'm going to send an agent to get your phone and computer so we can pick up where Sergeant Moss left off," Hiller said, using Pete's special forces title.

"Anything you need. Thank you for helping me."

Shay and Roman left Pete and Hiller to go over more details. When they got to the elevator, Roman hit the up button to call it. Shay's gaze was on the floor, arms crossed over her chest.

"Good job in there," he said, wanting to break the silence.

She nodded but didn't say anything, and one hand swiped at her cheek.

His heart skipped a beat. "Hey." He stepped closer and tilted her chin so she'd look up at him. "This is going to be over soon." *As soon as I get within ten feet of the piece of shit who's making you cry.*

Her golden eyes glowed through the tears, and she nodded again.

"Come here." He reached out, and she folded into him. Her forehead rested on his shoulder, his whole world in his arms.

The elevator pinged next to them, and its doors opened. She pulled away and wiped her face as she stepped inside. "Thanks." The door started to close. "I'm so sorry about all of this."

He thrust out a hand to stop it. Gripping the cold metal kept him from stepping inside and scooping her back into his arms. "None of this is your fault. You have nothing to be sorry about."

A pair of women appeared at the end of the hallway. "Oh, hold that elevator," one of them called.

Roman glanced from them to Shay and stepped back, letting the door close.

Shay wiped her face and mouthed, "Thank you", before disappearing behind the steel.

The women reached him, and one glared. "Excuse me, sir. You do work here, don't you?"

Sighing, he turned to them. "Yeah. I do."

She sneered. "And didn't you hear me ask to hold the elevator?"

"I did."

"I thought so. What's your name? I'm going to file a complaint."

"Be my guest. Roman. That's R-O-M-A-N."

Recognition crossed the friend's face. She grabbed the woman's arm and shook her head.

He pointed down the hall. "My office is the third on the left. Slide the complaint under the door." He stalked off as the friend explained in a low voice who he was.

The woman's apology carried down the hall, and he raised a hand waving it away. The novelty of being an on-site celebrity didn't appeal to him.

He flung open his office door and grabbed his gym bag.

Time to hit something.

****

Two days went by, and Roman barely crossed paths with Shay. He caught glimpses of her heading to the hiking trails or sitting in the sun, and his heart would lurch. It killed him to stay away from her. It killed him more that she seemed to be content with his staying away.

Tuesday morning, Pete knocked on Roman's office door. "Hey. Hiller wants me to call him."

Hope sparked in Roman's chest, and he ushered

him in, shutting the door as Pete set his laptop on the desk.

"Ready?" Pete's hand hovered above the call button.

Roman nodded and perched on the edge of one of the chairs facing the desk.

Pete pushed the button, and they exchanged greetings when Hiller's image filled the screen.

Hiller cleared his throat. "We're still working on getting something concrete to link Kyle to one of the murdered prostitutes, but we have a new concern." Roman's hope deflated with each word. "A girl, Valerie Morton, went missing from the Portland Hampstead Saturday. They just recovered her body. It was badly beaten, assaulted, and strangled. The hotel's security camera system was hacked. The video feed was erased for the entire week leading up to the day she disappeared, but she told one of her coworkers her date was picking her up in a Lexus. And another worker remembers her flirting with a customer matching Kyle's description."

"Where is he?" Roman's voice was flat.

"I have agents watching him twenty-four-seven, and right now he's at a restaurant downtown eating brunch alone."

"And there's no sign that he's figured out Shay's here?"

"No. We had a near-incident when the rookie we sent to pick up Shay's phone plugged it in to charge on his way back. He didn't realize it would power on automatically, but it doesn't look like Kyle noticed. I'm keeping agents on him until we have enough to pick him up."

"How close are you?" Roman tried to keep the frustration from his voice.

"The best link we have is that the previous bodies, along with Valerie, were beaten and killed by someone left-handed, which Kyle is. And his travel dates match the timing of the murder in California. We're coordinating with the appropriate agencies, but so far, they're having the same luck. There's not enough to back the warrant for his DNA yet, and the witness from the hotel picked the wrong guy from a picture lineup. We've been scanning cameras at intersections around the area, but so far nothing."

"He probably got right on the highway." That's what made Roman pick the Hampstead in the first place—it was right next to an on-ramp.

"That seems likely at this point. I have a team getting surveillance camera footage from the gas stations and fast-food cameras at exits both north and south, but it's going to take some time."

"Okay, thanks for letting us know." A headache brewed behind Roman's eyes.

"Least I can do. If this is what it looks like, this guy should have been on our radar a long time ago. We will get him."

Agent Hiller's promise echoed in Roman's mind as he hung up.

Chapter 20

Kyle

Kyle fought to keep his steps from his car to his front door even and slow, just like he'd struggled to keep from speeding on the drive home. He had to appear to be as normal and carefree as possible since someone was watching. Right after leaving brunch, he'd glanced in the rearview mirror and saw the same non-descript beige sedan that had been behind him earlier in the day. He turned, and the sedan continued on its way, but the black Ford two cars back made the same turn.

Kyle rolled to a stop at a crosswalk and waved for a mom with two little kids to cross. He smiled and nodded as they passed by, one of the kids waving.

He drove through the intersection and took the next left. The Ford stayed straight, but Kyle kept one eye on his mirrors as he drove. At the next intersection, the beige sedan pulled out from a parking spot and took its place three cars back from him.

Fuck.

It was an exquisite torture to deny himself from pressing the gas pedal to the floor. Instead, he kept to the speed limit, slowed down for all yellow lights, and stopped at the post office for stamps he didn't need. Mundane. Normal. Nothing to let on he knew.

Meanwhile, in his mind, he recited each of the car's license plates like a mantra.

It wasn't until he was inside his townhouse that he let his composure slip and took the stairs two at a time down to the basement. He chucked the envelope containing the stamps into the trash and flipped the switch to power up the bank of monitors on his wraparound desk. His fingers flew over the keys as he searched the police database for the plate numbers. Nothing. He let out a deep sigh and collapsed into his desk chair.

If it wasn't cops, there was still a chance it was a tail. It wouldn't be the first time the media or one of his dad's political opponents tried to find something unsavory on Kyle to use against his dad.

Kyle entered the first plate in the civilian database, and it came up right away as registered to a tax company. Kyle frowned. Not a PI agency and not a news outlet. He entered the second one and came up with the same tax company. His palms began to sweat.

He opened a search window and looked up the address to find it was real. The company website was barebones, but it existed. Kyle took the last step and traced the IP address that registered the website.

"Fuck!" he yelled, standing so fast his chair tipped over.

FBI.

He paced the room combing his hands through his hair. He'd been so careful with the moron from the hotel. Where did he leave tracks? The girl in Baltimore? She'd almost escaped and had made a lot of noise before he caught up to her, but they'd been in the middle of the woods. No one should have been around for miles, and there was nothing to trace back to him anyway...

A cold realization struck him. It had to be Shay. That explained why she was so hard to find. She hadn't tried to access her email or bank accounts, and he hadn't found so much as a hint of her popping up anywhere. There was no way she'd disappeared so completely without help. If only he still had access to her phone. He'd stopped trying to track it days ago. She wasn't stupid and wouldn't turn it on again.

He paused mid-stride. Or would she? He ran to where he'd flung his backpack to the floor days ago and yanked out the iPad inside. It powered on as he walked to his desk. Hunched over, he didn't even bother to right the chair so he could sit. He swiped into the app that monitored her phone and went through the log. Two days ago, the phone had turned back on for a few minutes. He typed in the coordinates it gave him and found it on a map. It was on a road about forty miles northwest of Portland. The last location recorded before the phone had turned off again was three miles south of the original point.

Kyle spent the rest of the afternoon systematically plugging every nearby house, gas station, supermarket, and even a rest area into a search engine looking for anything that stood out.

He almost missed it. It was a road that seemed to dead end, but a slip of his mouse showed an inhabited island that turned out to be a resort. One website later, a waterfall of rage and excitement washed over him as Roman's cocky face stared back at him from the screen.

"Bravo." He clapped in the solitude of his basement. That performance Roman had put on in his truck...he'd pulled one over on Kyle. Not something that happened often. And it wouldn't happen again.

Kyle stared at the computer screen and clicked onto the resort's main page. There would be no more underestimating. He bit into his lip as he began to plan, savoring the taste of copper.

Chapter 21

Shay

Shay's reluctance to take advantage of the resort's amenities dissipated as she got used to the idea that she'd be on the island for a while. Pete had assured her there was nothing she could do for the moment but wait. And unless she kept herself occupied, intrusive memories of how easy conversations with Roman used to flow constantly invaded her thoughts.

To keep busy, she'd spent the past few days taking yoga classes, hiking, swimming in the lake. Anything to avoid Roman avoiding her. To be around him knowing he'd settled down with someone else cut like a dull knife. His cool demeanor when she first arrived on the island had now become cold.

After an early morning swim, she caught her breath as she walked across the beach to her towel, still dripping. She wrapped the towel around herself and checked the time on the watch she'd gotten from the gift shop since she no longer had a phone. Seven a.m. on Thursday. She consulted the folded activity schedule that had been left on her pillow during last night's turn down service. The first activity was at nine—Zumba. So not her thing. She yawned and stretched out in the sun. Maybe she'd just stay on the beach all morning.

The peaceful moment was short-lived as the hairs

on the back of her neck began to prickle. It was a skill all good waitresses developed, an ESP that could tell you a table's eyes were burning a hole in your back when you were too busy to look. Someone was looking.

She pulled on her shorts with shaking hands, grabbed her towel and bag, and headed into the woods to the trail that led back to the hotel. It was a straighter shot than the paved path for the carts. She quickened her steps while glancing over her shoulder, and a flicker of movement caught her eye. One of the hotel staff had paused his task of setting up the lounge chairs on the beach to look her way.

You're losing it, Shay.

He waved with a friendly smile, and she almost laughed in relief. Then she caught a whiff of peppery cologne that made her blood run cold. She could never mistake the scent. It was Kyle's exact brand, and no hotel employee would pay whatever insane amount he did on cologne. She broke into a slow jog, careful to watch her footing over the rocks and roots in the path as her mind searched for a rational answer. This resort catered to Kyle's demographic. One of the other guests probably just happened to use the same cologne. That thought didn't stop her jog from breaking into a full run until she broke from the trees onto the far side of the lawn from the hotel.

"Shay!" The yell came from her left, and she stopped in her tracks as she recognized the concierge's voice.

"Good morning, Manuel," she called, panting as he strode over.

"Is everything okay?" His eyebrows knit together.

"Oh, yeah. Just taking a little jog." She put her

hands on her hips, still trying to catch her breath.

His eyes momentarily flicked to her flip-flops before saying, "Lovely morning for it. I'm glad I caught you. I have a few complimentary spa passes for you at the desk. Come by whenever you are free."

"Oh, thanks. That's really nice of you."

"Chef suggested it, actually."

Roman. Her heart sank. He was pushing her toward another thing she could do with no chance of running into him. She was already keeping her distance. How much more did he want?

They parted, and she walked back to the main hotel, hoping there'd be news today from Agent Hiller that they'd arrested Kyle and she could leave. She could no longer fool herself into thinking all she had was a crush. It was a constant ache in her heart pulling her toward Roman, and no matter how much she liked Gisella, this was turning into torture. She'd met Gisella for lunch one other time, and the fact Shay genuinely had fun with her made it worse. Feeling too much like a traitor, she'd declined all Gisella's further attempts to hang out.

Shay walked into the Great Hall and glanced toward reception. She slowed, coming to a dead stop. Usually, the desk was bookended by tasteful and understated floral arrangements. Today there were two bouquets of pale pink roses in full bloom.

A sense of foreboding crept up Shay's spine as she walked toward the smiling attendant.

"Good morning, Ms. Cole. What can I do for you?"

"Hi. I can't help but notice these flowers are different from the usual ones."

"Yes, some mix-up at the florist. They're going to

bring the right ones tomorrow. If you want one of these, we can send them to your room when the new arrangements arrive."

"NO." The force of her answer startled the receptionist, and Shay lowered her voice. "Thank you, but I'm all set. Do you know where Roman is?"

First the cologne then the flowers—maybe small coincidences, but when Kyle was involved, there was no such thing as coincidences, so far.

"I can have him paged."

Shay spotted Pete across the room as he walked out the front door. She shook her head at the receptionist. "No, it's okay. Thanks."

She rushed to catch up with Pete and called his name when she was close enough to not disturb the other guests.

"Hey, Shay." He turned and came to a stop on the porch. "What's up?"

"Nothing really. I'm just a little antsy today. Have you checked in with Agent Hiller recently?"

"Not for a couple days, but I can if you'd like?"

"If you don't mind. It would make me feel better."

"No problem. Is everything okay?"

"Yeah, everything is fine. I'm just being paranoid today."

"Understandable. But humor me and tell me what set it off."

"This morning at the beach I felt like I was being watched and smelled the same cologne Kyle wears. Now, the order of flowers for the front desk got mixed up, and the florist brought pink roses instead of what they ordered. Kyle brought me pink roses on our first date." Flustered hearing it out loud she added, "I'm sure it's nothing...never mind."

"Hold up." Pete held up a hand to stop her from leaving. He retraced his steps to the door and glanced toward reception. He ducked back out and gave her a reassuring smile. "No harm in checking in. I'll call now," he said, already pulling out his phone.

"Hi. This is Pete Moss. Do you still have eyes on Kyle?" There was a pause as he listened. "Could you do me a favor and check in with them, make sure he's still pinned down? We had a delivery of pink roses that we didn't order. Thanks."

Shay cringed at the mention of the pink roses. *What a stupid thing to be wasting their time with.*

After a few moments of silence, Pete perked up. "Okay, thanks. Talk to you soon."

He hung up and smiled at Shay. "Kyle's home, and the surveillance team saw him making breakfast ten minutes ago."

She let out a relieved sigh. "Thanks so much."

"Anytime," he said.

She resumed her original path back to her room, making a point of relaxing her shoulders as she went.

****

Shay spent most of the day sketching jewelry designs on hotel stationery to occupy her hands and mind. Even with Pete's reassurance, it felt less exposed to stay in the security of her room. Her stomach growled just after eight p.m., reminding her that she hadn't eaten since she'd ordered room service that morning. She stood and stretched the kinks out of her neck, then went down to Sueno. The Pub was more casual, but it would also be crowded at this time, while Sueno would, hopefully, be starting to empty out.

She asked for a table in the back. Even tucked away, she couldn't stop herself from stealing glances at Roman as he worked. The special was a sundried tomato risotto that reminded her of one of her favorite pasta dishes at George's. The balance in the risotto was even better than the pasta with each bite capturing the perfect amount of basil and just a hint of parmesan.

Every spoonful was a momentary comfort but did little to stop her from wishing Roman was sitting across from her. Behind the glass, he bit his bottom lip as he used tweezers to arrange a garnish on a plate. The ache in Shay's chest grew watching him, and she turned her eyes down to her empty plate.

Her waiter's voice startled her. "Can I get you anything else?"

She sucked in a breath and smiled, placing her napkin on the table. "No, thank you."

As she was getting up to leave, she glanced to the kitchen one last time. Roman caught her gaze, and he lit up with the same half-smile that he used to give her every morning. Her heart betrayed her and lurched into a gallop. That smile used to make her feel like she'd made his day just by coming to work. She gave a small wave, and the moment faded as he turned back to the plate he was inspecting.

Emotionally drained, she rode the elevator up to her room. The doors opened, and the unmistakable odor of Kyle's cologne surrounded her. Whoever was at the beach that morning must be staying on her floor. That thought didn't stop Shay from triple checking her door was locked, or later looking under the bed before tugging Roman's sweatshirt over her pajamas.

The uneasiness didn't settle, and she flicked on the

closet light to fish out her purse. Her hand dug through until it clasped her pocketknife, taking the edge off her anxiety. She set the knife on the nightstand and drifted off while reading in the soft glow from the bedside light.

Violent pounding on her door jolted her from a fitful sleep.

Instantly awake, she didn't fully panic until a man's voice yelled, "Open this door. Now!"

She kicked off her covers and flung herself toward the nightstand. Her trembling hand flailed for the knife, knocking the phone off its cradle and onto the floor in the process.

She sat up, heart pounding, with her fingers clenched around the tiny blade.

Before she could think what to do next, the door adjoining her room to the next burst open. Roman strode through with a baseball bat in hand. He flung the door to the hall open and swung the bat over his shoulder in one motion, ready to strike.

"What the hell," came the shocked voice from the other side.

"Back up," Roman yelled.

"I think I have the wrong room," the guy said with a slur.

Shay stood on shaky legs to get a look at him and make sure beyond a shadow of a doubt that it wasn't Kyle. The drunk guy swayed back and forth mumbling something about his girlfriend locking him out. *Not Kyle.*

"Sit." Roman pointed with the bat to the floor in the hallway.

He came back into her room, eyes flicking to hers

only for a second before he looked down and retrieved the phone from where it dangled off the nightstand.

He dialed, then pressed it to his ear. "A drunk guest just tried to kick in the door of room 508. Get security up here, now."

Hanging up, he turned to her and searched her eyes. "Are you okay?"

She nodded, still stunned he'd appeared from the next room.

"I have to go make sure he doesn't leave before security gets here. I'll be right back."

She nodded again, and he walked out of the room.

Shay's mind raced. Not Kyle. Just a drunk guy. Roman was in the room next door.

It only took a minute for security to get there and for Roman to come back in. He relocked the door and turned to her with his head down.

His expression was unreadable when he sighed and looked up. "It's late. Can we talk tomorrow?"

She cleared her throat with no idea where they would start anyway. "Yeah, okay."

He walked into the adjoining room, only to return moments later with a pillow and a blanket. He tossed them onto the floor between her bed and the door, then lay down pulling the blanket around himself.

"You're staying in here?" she asked, even though the answer seemed obvious.

"Pete told me about the flowers and the beach. I'll feel better being in here."

"Where's Gisella?"

"Home. But I promise I'll be a better bodyguard than her." A trace of laughter entered his voice. He rolled on his side and angled his head toward her.

"Would you mind shutting off the light?"

She pulled her feet up on the bed and reached over to click off the light. In the dark, the reassuring sound of him breathing next to her worked better than a lullaby. For the first time in months, she slept straight through to the morning.

It was such sound sleep that she didn't hear him leave. Instead, she woke to an empty room, with only the pillow and blanket on the floor as evidence that she hadn't imagined the whole thing.

Chapter 22

Roman

Jesus. He couldn't keep doing this. Last night had almost killed him. Lying feet from her as she slept, he'd had to stop himself from crawling into her bed and wrapping her in his arms. As if he hadn't invaded her space enough. Now, there was no way to deny he'd been secretly staying in the room next to her. She'd traded one stalker for another.

Roman continued to beat himself up through breakfast service. He wasn't even on the schedule to work, but he couldn't face Shay yet and snuck out before dawn. He was going to have to somehow explain that he forced his way into her room last night due to fierce protective instincts that he had no right to have. There was just no way he could have done anything else. Not after hearing that pounding on her door.

That pounding. Man, when that snapped him out of sleep, he was ready to kill Kyle. Already on edge from the issue with the flowers earlier, he'd been primed to react. The florist reassured Pete that it was a simple mix-up, and Hiller's men were still watching Kyle, but the possibility unnerved him. That drunk was lucky Roman noticed Shay was wearing his sweatshirt before he opened the door. It threw him off his warpath just enough that he looked before he swung.

He'd first hoped the sweatshirt was a sign there was some remnant of feelings stirring up in her. But that hope was dashed when it became clear she was uncomfortable with him there. She'd even asked for Gisella instead of him, and he still gave her no option. He hated himself.

He slammed a pan on a burner and his sous chef, Ricky, looked at him sideways, but said nothing. Roman had been in a pretty bad mood most days since Shay had arrived.

A line cook approached him as he cracked eggs into the pan. "Excuse me, Chef?"

"What?" Roman didn't look up.

"The produce order hasn't come in yet."

One of the yolks broke, and Roman yanked the pan off the burner and pitched it into a bus bin, sending the runny egg spattering over the side. He spun to face the cook. "What did they say when you called?"

"I haven't called yet," the young cook said, shrinking back.

Roman let the silence speak for him so he didn't say something he would regret.

"I'll go do it now." The cook slipped on the splattered egg in his rush to get away. Righting himself quickly, he hurried to the phone in the back of the kitchen.

Roman bent and cleaned up the mess before anyone else stepped in it, then tore off his apron. "I'm gonna take a break."

"Good idea." Ricky stepped in to take over for Roman, barking out the next order to be fired.

Needing to burn off some steam, Roman opened his office closet. He pulled out the replacement for the spare set of sweats that he'd loaned to Shay. While he changed, he tried to force his mind to think of anything other than the image of Shay wearing his clothes. He tied his sneakers too tight and left out a side door that led to the sunken garden. As soon as he stepped into the tree line, he took off running on the most challenging trail on the island. It was listed as Nightingale on the resort map but nicknamed "Nightmare" among the staff. Its initial steep ascent was followed by a sharp decline down to the lake. After a three-mile stretch along the water's edge, it shot back up the side of a cliff at an angle that would have had a grade warning if it were a road.

An hour later, he finished the five-and-a-half-mile loop with a personal best time. His legs burned from the grueling pace he'd kept over the steep and rough terrain. It had been a beautiful sunrise with the first rays of sun breaking through the tree cover and morning mist rising off the lake. None of that did anything to ease his mood. He was a coward for avoiding Shay. Being aware of that didn't change his plan to shower in the gym, so he wouldn't chance running into her in the hallway.

The whole run, he'd tried to come up with what he was going to say to her. He had to find some way to explain why he'd invaded her privacy by staying next door to her with a key to her room without telling her. Drenched and exhausted, he had no better idea than the one he'd started the run with. *I love you.*

Roman stepped out of the woods into the sunken garden and froze. She was directly ahead of him, sitting on the stone steps that led to the garden's lowest level. One hand hugged her knees to her chest, the other held a steaming mug. She stared across the grass, sparkling with morning dew, to where a group of swallows flitted in and out of a birdbath. She reached down and traded her coffee for a sketch pad then started to draw, pausing on and off to look toward the birds.

He only lingered a few moments to appreciate the look of deep concentration on her face as the sunlight caught the shades of red in her dark hair. Taking advantage of that concentration, he made his way around the side of the garden instead of going through it in case she caught him in her peripheral view. *Such. A. Coward.*

He stopped to grab clean clothes from his office before taking a cold shower in the gym.

When he walked into the main kitchen, he knew something was wrong as soon as he saw Ricky's face.

Ricky spoke before Roman had time to ask. "More orders aren't showing up."

"Which ones?" Roman winced, rubbing his forehead.

"All of them." The young cook's voice cracked as Roman's stare bore into him.

"How is that possible?"

"They were all canceled," he said, adding quickly, "We called to check."

A line cook chimed in, "That's impossible. Who would cancel all our orders leading into a weekend?"

Dammit. Kyle, that's who.

Roman turned around to walk right back out of the kitchen, directing his staff as he went. "Rework whatever you have to on the menu to get through today with what we have on hand. I'll take care of it."

"Yes, Chef," they responded in unison, as he

pushed through the swinging door. Not even nine in the morning yet, and it was already a bad day.

Roman pulled out his phone as he walked. He spoke as soon as Pete's groggy voice came through the line. "I need you to check our system for a hacker."

"Good morning to you, too."

"Someone canceled all our food orders for the weekend."

"Shit." Pete said.

"Yeah, shit." A familiar helplessness tightened his chest. If it was Kyle, he'd figured out Shay was here. "If you find anything, send it to Hiller."

"I'm on it." The line went dead as Pete hung up.

Roman went to the ground floor and entered the café. He ordered the largest coffee they served and a grilled cheese with bacon, his breakfast of choice to prepare for a rough day. He ate it in his office as he called vendors to try to get the orders resent. It was lucky he had a good relationship with so many of them. By noon, he'd re-ordered almost everything they needed for the busy weekend. Instead of being relieved, a sensation of dread crept up his spine.

Pete's name flashed on his phone screen, but Roman already knew what he was going to say. The flowers, now the orders being canceled—these attacks were getting less subtle. It could only mean one thing— Kyle was sending a message. He'd found them and didn't care if they knew it.

And this wasn't going to be the end.

Chapter 23

Shay

Shay counted to fifty under her breath to make sure Roman was gone before she threw her sketchpad onto the garden steps next to her and buried her head in her hands. She'd seen him as soon as he stepped out of the woods. He'd stopped dead in his tracks, then went out of his way to avoid her. She picked up her sketchpad and empty cup then went back inside. *So much for talking today.*

She went to the café to order something to take to her room and wallow. As she placed her order for an egg and cheese sandwich, Gisella materialized beside her, pulled her out of line, and said to the barista, "Cancel that order." To Shay, she said, "I'm so glad you haven't eaten. I'm starving. Give me five minutes to shower, and I will take to you to Farmstand for breakfast. You'll love it. I promise." She ran off with a yoga mat tucked under her arm before Shay could say no.

Shay took a deep breath and sank into a chair in the corner of the café that looked out to a small courtyard with ivy-draped walls and a waterfall fountain trickling down one wall. Other guests filtered in from the outdoor yoga class that had just ended. Gisella wasn't five minutes, but she also didn't take more than fifteen, making Shay wonder, again, how she managed to look so effortlessly perfect in jeans and a loose T- shirt.

Shay still wore the black leggings and tank top that she'd pulled on for comfort when she had decided to go sketch in the garden this morning. An oversized open-front light gray sweater completed the outfit. With flip-flops and a messy bun on top of her head she looked homeless compared to Gisella.

"Come on. You're in for a treat." Gisella pulled her out of the chair and hooked her arm through Shay's as they walked into the sunny courtyard. "I know you had a rough night. This will start your day on the right foot."

So, sometime between leaving Shay's floor and running through the woods, Roman found time to update Gisella.

Gisella led them to the nearest shuttle hut and teased the young employee as they drove about needing to see his ID. He glowed while on the receiving end of her attention.

After tipping the driver, Shay and Gisella entered Farmstand and were welcomed with warm greetings from servers in jeans and simple navy-blue aprons. They were led to a table against large windows overlooking the stream.

"This is beautiful." Shay looked around, admiring the simple décor. The wooden tables each had a small, clear, square vase with one or two multicolored daisies. Other than that, the only other pops of color were from vibrant green plants, hanging overhead. They hadn't needed to add much—the wooden interior was beautiful on its own in the sunlight, and the windows gave spectacular views of the stream and the forest beyond.

The menu was written on free-standing chalkboards. Shay was torn between the apple pancakes and the farmer's scramble with garlic roasted fingerling potatoes. When it came time to order, she made a last-minute change and ordered the NY Twist. It was a bagel with locally made cream cheese, thick slices of heirloom tomatoes, and capers.

Gisella ordered eggs Florentine. She smiled, rubbing her hands together as their waiter returned with a basket. "This is the best part."

She was right—it was freshly baked cinnamon rolls that melted in Shay's mouth. "Oh my God, these are incredible."

"You would have never thought Roman a baker, right?" Gisella licked frosting from a fingertip. "He sweet-talked my mom's recipe out of her after she made a batch when he was visiting. He's perfected it since then."

"Gisella." Shay needed to understand why Gisella didn't hate her. Her fiancé had brought another woman to invade their lives and hadn't been sleeping at home. "You know Roman's been staying in the room next to me?"

"He told me." She took another bite of her cinnamon roll.

"And you have no feelings about that?"

"Feelings?" Gisella frowned. "I think he should have told you so it wouldn't be a surprise, but he didn't want you to think it was creepy."

"How can that not bother you?" Shay said, exasperated.

"If I let it bother me every time Roman didn't listen to me, I would have pulled all my hair out years ago." She laughed, picking up her glass.

"Gisella, he's your fiancé. How can you be so nonchalant about all this?"

Gisella coughed on a sip of water. "Roman? My fiancé?" she sputtered from behind a napkin, still coughing. "Oh my God." She broke out laughing. "Pete is my fiancé. You thought I was with Roman? Is this why you started avoiding me?"

"What? Yes. Wait...what?" Shay stammered.

"Roman is my brother, well half-brother," Gisella said with barely contained amusement.

"This whole time?"

"Since I was nine, and he was born, yes. We share a dad who had terrible luck with women."

"How did I not know this?"

"I honestly have no idea." Gisella glanced over her shoulder and waved to their server.

"I've been feeling so guilty, thinking you were together," Shay confessed, relieved.

"Oh?" Gisella raised one eyebrow, a wicked smile on her lips. "And what are you guilty of?"

"Nothing's happened. I mean, nothing physical. I wouldn't have no matter who I thought he was with, but I really like you so there's no way." Shay's face flushed.

"But you want it to?" Gisella egged her on.

Shay said nothing, face on fire.

Gisella clapped her hands together. "I knew it. He told me you weren't interested in him, but I knew he was wrong. Anyone with eyes can see what's between you two." The waiter arrived, and Gisella ordered two glasses of champagne. "We're going to celebrate. This all makes so much sense now. He said you were distant with him, but of course you would be if you thought he was engaged."

"I just don't get it. He told me you both lived on the other side of the island."

"We do. There are a few houses scattered over there. We renovated two of them. Pete and I live in one and he lives, very much alone, in the other. God, he's so stupid. How could he let such a big misunderstanding happen with you of all people? It's such a Roman thing to do, fall for a girl for the first time in his adult life and let her think he's engaged to someone else. Idiot." She shook her head.

"From what I was told he's fallen for a lot of girls," Shay said, as the waiter arrived and set long-stem glasses on the table.

"He went out with a lot of girls, but he's been hung up on you since he met you. I never thought I'd see it," Gisella said, as the waiter uncorked the bottle and poured two glasses. "Cheers! To my idiot brother." Gisella held out her glass for Shay to clink.

She sipped the pale liquid, savoring the crisp hint of melon and the bubbles on her tongue before swallowing. Skeptical of Gisella's take, Shay sighed. "Everyone said he was a real player."

"It could seem that way. I think it was more he was looking for something that he didn't know how to find, and when you started at George's, your name came up more and more. The other girls just faded away." More seriously, she continued, "When we got him released from ICE and he found out you were gone he was beside himself. He looked. He had Pete look. He hired private detectives. He was so broken, not knowing if you were safe. That was when I knew for sure you were different for him."

Gisella's words and the champagne lifted a weight off Shay's shoulders. They ordered another glass, then another as they laughed and talked. Gisella told her about meeting Pete when he was assigned to her security detail. When she bought the resort, she asked Pete to come be head of security, and he asked her to marry him.

"I can see why you wanted to live here. It's really beautiful."

"It's held a special place in my heart since coming here as a child. Now, it's my retirement plan since I'm the ripe old age of thirty-seven."

"Thirty-seven?" Shay was genuinely shocked. She knew Gisella was nine years older than Roman. She just never thought what that actually made Gisella's age.

"I know, geriatric in model years," Gisella joked.

"No. I meant you don't look older than twenty-four."

"Good genes." Gisella waved away the compliment and sipped the last of her champagne. "If we stay any longer, I'm going to order another, and I'll have to be carried home." She folded her napkin and placed it on the table.

"Gisella, thank you," Shay said, as they stepped out of the building into bright sunshine.

"Well, I hope now you'll stop turning down my invitations. I could use a friend here. And I could definitely use a nap after all that champagne." She gave Shay a hug before heading down the path to her house.

Shay turned and started toward the resort, wanting to walk rather than take a cart. So, Roman wasn't taken. It opened doors in Shay's mind that she thought had closed forever. As she went, the bounce in her steps faded. He wasn't taken, but he'd made it pretty clear since she'd arrived that he wasn't interested in her. At George's, he flirted with her non-stop and went out of his way to spend every free second at work with her. For the past week, he barely seemed to tolerate her. She could never pay him back for what he was doing for her, but that was the kind of guy he was. He'd probably do the same for anyone. It was more hopeless than if he did have a fiancée.

Lost in thought, she almost ran into Pete on the front steps to the main hotel.

"Sorry, Shay. Things have gotten a little nuts here." Pete looked up from his phone.

"Why? What happened?"

"Our friendly neighborhood hacker." Pete sighed. "He canceled all the food orders this morning, and we just found he has some type of automated system running on multiple travel sites giving us poor reviews."

"Oh, no." Her heart sank. He knew she was here.

"Don't stress it." He glanced at her face, and his voice softened. "The FBI is watching him day and night. He can't hurt you."

Guilt overrode any fear for the moment. "That doesn't seem to stop him from hurting the resort. I shouldn't be here."

"Nonsense. It's an inconvenience at best. Roman fixed the orders already, and our clientele is mostly word of mouth. We have a very strong community of guests who wouldn't believe the trash he's writing. Plus, I'll have it all taken down as soon as I get to the main security office. Go enjoy the day." He looked back at his phone as he jogged down the stairs and around the side of the building.

Dark clouds had been gathering, and thunder rumbled in the distance. *Perfect.* She rushed inside to hide in her room and pull the covers over her head.

Chapter 24

Roman

Roman had taken a golf cart over to his house to grab a spare pair of shoes. On top of the fun surprises Kyle had set up for him, he'd also managed to have a new cook spill a tub of salsa on him when he checked to make sure things were running okay in the kitchen. He had plenty of clothes to change into in his hotel room, but the only pair of shoes he had, besides his now tomato-filled sneakers, were his kitchen clogs, and there was no way he could go to the gym in those later.

The only upside to avoiding Shay was that he was in the best shape of his life. He usually ran once or twice a week but since she had been here, he'd gone every day. Plus, he put in way more hours than usual in the gym, devoting most of that time to beating the crap out of the heavy bag while imagining it was Kyle Matthews.

He pulled out of the woods near Farmstand, feeling like a dork puttering around the island at seven miles an hour with a quiet electric hum instead of the revving of a real engine. Gisella had been firm about avoiding anything motorized besides emergency vehicles to maintain the peace and serenity of the island. Her exact words to him were, "it's a luxury resort, not motocross." At least she'd let him get a stash of four-wheelers for when he absolutely needed to get somewhere fast.

In front of his cart, Gisella appeared in the middle of the path, waving to him.

He slowed as he approached her, taking in her ear-to-ear grin. When she hugged him enthusiastically, the scent of alcohol wafted off her.

"Are you drunk?"

"Drunk…happy…Roman, I have the best news."

"Okay, get in. I'll drive you home so you don't get mowed down by one of these jalopies. I could use some good news." He turned the cart around and started back the way he came.

"Shay thought you and I have been together all this time."

"What do you mean?"

"Together, like dating, and then engaged together. Apparently, you never told her I was your sister, and she's been wandering through this week with a broken heart, trying to not let you see."

His heart skipped more beats than could be healthy. "She said that to you?" The question caught in his throat.

"Not in so many words, but Roman, she's clearly as head over heels for you as you are for her. When I told her she was different for you than the other girls you have dated, you should have seen her face."

He wished he had but not now, not with so much at stake. His frustration at the day welled up. "That wasn't your place. Why couldn't you just leave it alone?"

"For what? For you to deny your feelings for her until she gives up because she thinks you're not interested? She knows you've been avoiding her."

"Yeah, I'm avoiding her, Gisella. You think now is the time I should try to force a relationship on her? She's basically a prisoner here, and you don't think that may influence her decision? You don't think I want to tell her how I feel? It's all I think about. I can't risk putting it out there and having it ruined because of all this bullshit with Kyle. I won't chance losing her again, so stay out of it." He was breathing heavily by the time he finished.

They rolled to a stop in front of her house, and Gisella sat completely still. She turned toward him in stunned silence. Roman felt like a complete asshole as her eyes teared up. That is until she burst into a smile, clasping her hands together in front of her lips. "My baby brother, in love." She fanned her eyes.

"Oh my God. Get out!" he said, unable to suppress the smile spreading across his face.

She did as he requested but didn't walk away. "Roman, I really like her."

Me, too. He pointed toward her house. "Go. Take a nap, and no more talking about me to Shay."

He pulled away, making sure she was inside before he pressed the gas all the way down and cursed when the speedometer didn't break ten miles per hour.

Chapter 25

Kyle

It was all almost too easy. Kyle sat in the comfort of his room, four doors down from Shay's. He'd finally gotten access to the resort's internal security system. Once he was in, the first thing he did was open the resort's main email account, find this week's order confirmations from the food vendors, and cancel them. The head of security, Peter Moss, was better than he looked. It had taken Kyle longer than expected to tiptoe around the traps in the system that would alert them to his presence. And it had proven to be impossible to hack the system from outside, which both impressed Kyle and sped up his need to physically get to the resort. But things had gone smoothly yesterday.

****

Occasionally, over the past few years, it had been useful to have a body double. To find one, Kyle messed with the parameters of a widely used facial recognition program. He set it to search images for similarities instead of exact matches, then ran that program through local acting agencies' headshots. Using images of his own face for a search, he found Jace.

Jace was a close match in height, weight, and coloring. He also happened to be in enough debt that he was happy to be hired by Kyle on retainer. It was a monthly salary that was more than the guy usually made in six months. All he had to do was be willing to drop what he was doing at any time to stand in for Kyle, maintain and match his hair and body to Kyle's, plus some minor cosmetic surgery that, if anything, improved his overall aesthetic.

Jace had also proven himself quick on his feet. Last month, when Kyle sent him for a weekend at Sanctuary, Jace was supposed to steal Roman's laptop. Finding that he worked on an old-fashioned, and more conspicuous to take, desktop computer, Jace had instead returned with the wallet. Keeping Kyle's plan intact.

When Kyle was ready to make his way to the resort, he called Jace from a burner phone, and within an hour Jace had shown up posing as a food delivery guy. Kyle answered the door, pretended he needed to get his wallet, and had Jace step inside. There they quickly swapped shirts, and Kyle donned the dark wig and baseball hat Jace had come in with. It was less than thirty seconds and Kyle was out the door, counting a fistful of dollars while the actor made himself comfortable on the couch, opening take-out containers. Kyle took Jace's car and drove to the storage unit where he kept a variety of useful items, including spare electronics and a few changes of clothes.

The next hurdle occured when he got to the parking lot for the resorts ferry. His original plan was to blend in once there was a crowd, but security was scrutinizing everyone's room confirmations and IDs. *Paranoid much?* He laughed to himself and sat back to wait for the right opportunity to present itself. Patience was a virtue.

When a family with two young kids walked past struggling to manage the stroller and bags while one of the kids screamed bloody murder, Kyle pulled on his baseball cap and stepped out of his car. He fought the urge to scratch his neck where the ends of the dark wig poked out of the cap and blinked his irritated eyes. The first thing he'd do when he got to his room would be to take out the colored contacts. For now, he put the discomfort to the back of his mind and took long strides to retrace the family's steps. The parents hadn't noticed, but the kid only started screaming after a well-worn giraffe had toppled out of the stroller.

Kyle bent to scoop it up and circled back to get his own bags. He walked slowly so by the time he reached the dock, the family was through the security check.

A man stopped him as soon as he set foot on the dock. "Room confirmation and ID."

Kyle tucked the giraffe under his arm and smiled. "Of course." He pulled up the confirmation on his phone and handed it over. Kyle made a show of checking his pockets for his wallet as the kid's screams escalated enough that the security guard glanced at the family.

"Sorry," Kyle said, holding up the giraffe. "It's my nephew's. He forgot it in the car, and he'll be inconsolable without it. Can I run it over to him and come back? I think I packed my wallet, so it's going to take me a minute to dig it out." Kyle pointed down to the oversized suitcase next to him.

The guard shook his head and waved to the family. "Just go. My kid was the same way at that age."

Kyle jogged toward the stroller holding out the giraffe. The kid squealed in delight, and Kyle made a big show of handing it over then offered to help carry one of the bulky bags that the dad was struggling to manage along with their suitcases. The group got on the boat one big happy family, and Kyle struck up a conversation with the father about his golf game after noticing a famous club's logo on his shirt.

They were laughing like old friends when they stepped off the ferry at the other end and didn't part ways until they passed the second security guard, eyeballing each passenger as they disembarked onto the island. The front desk was his last real hurdle, but he checked in without an issue. He didn't want to chance the fake ID he brought with scrutiny from the security at the dock, but the front desk guy barely even glanced at it. On the way from the ferry to the hotel, Kyle hadn't noticed any security measures that seemed over the top. They weren't expecting him yet. It probably helped that anyone who had a reason to care would think he was still home in Portland.

Since arriving on the island, Kyle had periodically checked the security camera at his house. As always, Jace was following his instructions to a tee. Right now, if the FBI cared to look, Jace was sprawled across the couch eating a bowl of cereal. Kyle wasn't sure if they were bugging his phone or house, so he told Jace not to make any phone calls in case they noticed the voice was off. But he did give him a few girls' numbers to text with saying he had a cold. It set up a good excuse for him to stay home for a few days. Jace made sure to leave the front shades open and spend a good amount of time in the rooms the men surveilling him could see from the street. *Idiots.*

Now, Kyle had one more surprise for Roman to set

in motion, then he would start preparing to wait for Shay in her room tonight. He'd swiped a maid's all-access key card just after he arrived yesterday, then made sure to swipe the same maid's key card today since she hopefully wouldn't report it missing the second time to avoid looking incompetent. This evening he tested them both on his door and found, as he suspected, the key from yesterday was disabled but today's worked. *Too easy.* As soon as Shay left for dinner, he could let himself into her room.

It was the same plan he was going to use at the Hampstead: inject the paralytic then put her in a suitcase and walk out like any other guest carting luggage around. As long as she was back from dinner before nine-thirty they could make the last ferry to the mainland at ten. If not, he'd brought along enough of the drug to last until they could leave in the morning. Not his first choice, but they would have a fun night together even if she didn't remember it.

It was excruciating to sit in front of his laptop, waiting for her to pop up on the video feed. She finally showed up on the elevator bank camera at eight-thirty, and Kyle tracked her path on the cameras until she entered the main restaurant downstairs. *Showtime.*

He closed his laptop and slid it into his backpack. He'd carry that bag along with the empty suitcase to Shay's room in case he needed to leave fast, but for now, he took his time changing clothes, styling his hair, brushing his teeth, and spraying his chest with cologne. As he walked the four doors down to her room, he didn't care if she ate quickly or slowly. Either way, within hours he would finally have her. It was almost more anticipation than he could take.

In her room, he set up his laptop. He had added a motion sensor trigger on the elevator bank screen to alert him when someone got off on the fifth floor.

Sinking into a chair, he pulled out his phone, flicking to the breaking news app, and searched the headlines to see if his parting gift to Roman had been discovered yet.

Chapter 26

Shay

Exhaustion hit Shay after the drunken brunch with Gisella. The paranoia over the front desk's floral arrangement didn't help. She curled up in bed as soon as she got to her room. Hours later, the steady patter of rain on her window woke her. The last thing she remembered was taking a couple of ibuprofen for the champagne-induced headache that was coming on.

Her stomach growled, reminding her that she hadn't eaten since brunch. She stood, stretching her arms overhead and shaking off the last remnants of sleep before getting ready to go downstairs. She went for comfort and tugged on the flat ankle boots that were her favorite footwear that Gisella had picked out.

On the way to Sueno, intrusive thoughts about Roman continued to plague her. Nothing had changed even if he was single. He still didn't want her like she wanted him to. She never thought they were going to have some fairy tale romance when she believed Gisella was his fiancée, and she didn't think it was going to happen now. There was nothing she could do.

All that didn't help in the least when she walked into Sueno and picked out his broad shoulders though the glass to the kitchen. Her traitorous heart leapt. She wished nothing more than to be back in George's kitchen with Roman's deep blue eyes sparking as he made some comment about spending his life with her. The loss was so strong it ached.

"Good evening, Ms. Cole. Table for one?" The hostess welcomed her.

"I think I'll just take something to go," Shay replied, wishing she'd ordered room service.

"Excellent. Would you like to see a menu?"

"No thanks. I'll take whatever the special is." There was no doubt that it would be amazing. Even though the menu looked incredible, the specials had all been reminiscent of some of her favorite dishes Roman used to make at George's. If she couldn't go back to the past, at least she could have a taste of it.

"It should be ready shortly. Would you like to wait at the bar?"

"No," Shay said quickly. No reason to encourage the champagne headache to return. "I'll wait in the main hall."

She left and plopped onto one of the oversized chairs near reception. Out the window, the rain had slowed to a drizzle, but the wind had picked up, promising the storm wasn't over yet.

From the reception desk, a raised voice caught her attention. Carmen, the manager of guest services was usually cool and composed. But right now, her hushed tones didn't disguise the angry edge to her tone as she reprimanded the three receptionists on duty. Shay glanced around at the otherwise deserted area and strained to listen.

"...and if I find out it was one of our staff, you will not just be fired. You'll be prosecuted for violating the confidentiality agreement you signed. This is the kind of breach that could sink a hotel of our level."

Manuel approached with quick strides and pulled Carmen to the side. Their voices were too low to make out, but whatever he said seemed to calm her.

Shay waited until Carmen stepped away before approaching the front desk. The staff was visibly shaken, but Manuel's deep frown instantly transformed into a smile when he saw Shay. "Hello, my dear. How can I help you this evening?"

"Hi. What happened?"

"Nothing you need to be concerned with. I don't know if you're aware, but there's hot apple cider and fresh-baked cookies in the library. It's a nice dreary evening to curl up with a good book." His smile didn't reach his eyes.

Shay glanced to where he was wringing his hands, then back to his face. "Please. I need to know."

His smile faded back into a frown, and he sighed. "It will be news by morning. There's been a security breach. Someone leaked the files where we store our most sensitive client information."

Her heart sank. "What kind of information?"

"Personal phone numbers, addresses, credit card information." He flinched as he spoke. "It's already circulating on social media past the point of containment."

"Oh my God." Carmen was right; this would ruin the resort. Their whole image was based around discretion and privacy.

"Yes. It's very, very bad. We've already started to have cancelations, and it's barely been an hour."

Shay glanced toward the front door. She couldn't do this anymore. She'd put a target on their backs by being here, and now Roman and Gisella were paying the price. She had to go. The dock staff could call her a cab, and she'd go back to Lake Placid. If Kyle wanted to keep harassing her, she was going to make sure it was only her who suffered from now on.

"Shay? Are you okay?" Manuel asked.

She snapped back to attention. "What time is it?"

Manuel glanced at his computer monitor. "Nine forty-five."

She'd have to run to catch the last ferry at ten.

"Thank you, Manuel. Please tell Roman and Gisella I'm sorry this happened."

Shay took off for the front door at a fast pace that turned into an all-out sprint when she found the shuttle hut unmanned and all the carts gone. The rain had picked up and was driven in sheets by the force of the wind.

Worry about drying off later.

Her feet pounded along the path as she ran headfirst into the storm.

Chapter 27

Roman

Shay's dinner was the last order Roman filled. He tugged off his chef coat and left through the back of the kitchen as it was being boxed up for her. He had to go make sure everything with the data breach was still under control. For at least the tenth time since the clients' info was leaked, Roman thought about how grateful he was to Gisella for bringing Pete into their business. Pete had anticipated Kyle would try to hack into their computer system eventually since he kept hitting them electronically. The resort's security team had taken a number of steps in the past few days to make sure he couldn't do any real damage if he did succeed and get in.

One of those steps happened to be taking all sensitive client information out of the system and storing it on drives that were locked up in the vault. Pete had taken the additional precaution of populating their entire online system with addresses and phone numbers for a popular donut chain with locations across the country. Roman smirked, remembering the rationale Pete had given, that he'd always been a bagel man. Funny or not, he'd done a thorough job. Credit card numbers were made up, and upcoming reservation dates were falsified. The correct information was stored on the computer at the front desk which had been taken offline.

So far, no one had publicly announced the list was fake. The most exclusive clients had been personally called by Gisella or one of her assistants to alert them that their information was in fact still protected due to the extreme security measures that Sanctuary's security team had the foresight to take. Kyle could enjoy thinking his little trick worked for a while, but any bad press would be temporary. If all went well, the resort would be painted as a victim-turned-hero for helping to catch him.

Roman stopped at his office to lock up for the night before he made his way to Pete. When he stepped back into the hallway a few minutes later, Manuel was striding down the hall.

Roman took one look at his face and knew something was wrong. "What happened?"

"I've been looking for you. I'm worried about Ms. Cole."

"Why? What happened?" Roman asked again, with more force.

"She heard about the leaked data and took off into the rain."

No. His stomach dropped. "Took off? To go where?"

"She didn't say, but she asked the time before she left. My guess is, she's trying to make the ferry."

"It's canceled because of the weather." Roman furrowed his brow.

"I didn't have time to tell her that before she ran out," Manuel said, then added, "she seemed determined."

"How long ago did she leave?" Outside the wind howled.

"Ten minutes, maybe fifteen."

Roman ran across the ground floor and out the door that led to the shuttle parking lot. He grabbed a set of keys from the board they hung on. Not slowing down when he reached the golfcarts, he jogged past them to a four-wheeler, jamming the key into the ignition. He could make up all the lost time if he took side trails instead of the main paved road that she was probably on. Ignoring the sting of the rain on his face, he went as fast as the engine could take him across the lawn.

Leaning forward to crouch over the handlebars, he hit the dirt trail and slowed just enough to keep control as the four-wheeler bounced over rocks and roots. He tried not to let his thoughts wander to the possibility that she found a way off the island. There were tender boats. They kept the keys inside the boathouse, and staff often forgot to lock it. *No. She can't disappear again.*

He roared out of the woods, pushing the throttle as far as it would go, and landed on the paved trail for the last fifty feet to the boathouse.

A lone figure stood on the dock in the rain, and all his breath came whooshing back into his lungs.

"Shay," he yelled, not bothering to shut the engine off as he climbed off and jogged to her.

She turned around, crying. "Don't!" She held out a hand to keep him away. "I need to leave. I'm ruining your life."

Ignoring her outstretched arm, he cut the distance between them in two strides and cupped her face in his hands. "You are my life."

He gave up on any attempt at holding his feelings back and kissed her with every ounce of the passion that had built in him since her first day at George's. The sweetness of her lips mingled with her tears, and she melted against him, wrapping her fingers into the soaked cloth of his shirt.

Breathless, she pulled away, but Roman kept his forehead on hers.

Barely above a whisper, she said, "I don't want you to get hurt."

The thought of how close he'd come to losing her again brought the pin pricks of tears to his eyes. "Then, please, don't leave."

She nodded, her breath catching on a sob right before he brought his mouth against hers again. She wound her arms around his neck, pulling him closer. He pressed her back against the boathouse wall.

A crack of thunder broke the moment, and a gust of wind snaked itself around them.

His palms trailed down her arms, and he held onto one of her hands. "Come with me." He led her back to the waiting four-wheeler while the storm whipped itself into a frenzy.

Wordlessly, she climbed on, wrapped her arms around him, and rested her cheek against his back. A whole new breed of anxiety struck him like a shot of adrenaline. He'd done the exact thing he'd promised himself he wouldn't do. There'd been no concern about her vulnerability or the fact that she'd reached a dead end. He'd forced her to choose him.

He steered the four-wheeler onto the main path and turned in the opposite direction of the resort, clenching the handlebars.

I just ruined everything.

Chapter 28

Shay

Shay clung to Roman while they rode through the storm. The cold droplets were no match for the warmth radiating from his skin. Beneath her hands, his torso was reassuringly solid. Their kiss on the dock had erased all the misery that had been weighing her down. As they drove farther away from the hotel, the twinge of uncertainty for what would happen next was beaten down by the reassurance that she was with him, and she tightened her grip.

They turned off the path and rounded a corner, bringing them to a darkened house overlooking the lake. A motion light came on as they pulled up. Roman keyed in a code, and the garage door rumbled open. They pulled in to a typical garage, minus any cars. It wasn't any warmer than outside, but at least it was drier.

She climbed off the four-wheeler, instantly aware of the absence of his body against hers. She turned to him, planning to wrap her arms around his neck but paused when he swung his leg over the other side, putting the four-wheeler between them.

"Home sweet home," Roman said. His eyes darted away from hers, and he ran a hand over his short hair, flicking the water off. "Come with me. You must be freezing."

She bit her bottom lip and followed him through a door that hid a wooden staircase. He flipped on a bank of light switches and jogged up. When they emerged at the top of the stairs, she froze in awe.

The living room had cathedral ceilings and massive windows that faced the lake. A fireplace dominated one wall, and the open dining area flowed into a chef's kitchen. The overall design was rustic modern with hardwood floors, a refurbished table, and plain pendant lights dangling overhead in the kitchen and dining room.

A floating staircase led to the second floor, which was where Roman headed, calling back, "Up here."

At the top, a hallway opened to the floor below on one side and stretched past closed doors on the other. Roman pointed to a room as he passed but didn't slow. "Go right in there to shower and warm up. I'll find you some clothes."

She opened the door and found a simple guest room with an en suite bath. By the time she cranked on the water, she couldn't stop shivering. Under the steady stream she warmed up, and her irritation grew. How dare he kiss her like that and walk around like it never happened? He couldn't beg her to stay and not explain why he was acting this way.

She flipped off the tap and wrapped herself in a plush bath towel. In the guestroom, her clothes were now gone, but a pair of too big pajama bottoms and a soft T-shirt were folded on the bed waiting for her. She yanked the shirt over her head and rolled the pants waistband over twice to make them fit. If he thought they weren't going to talk about this, he had another thing coming.

She stepped into the hallway, fuming. The door at the very end was cracked open, and her bare feet padded down the hallway that overlooked the kitchen below. At his door, she raised her hand to knock, then dropped it. If he could barge into her room in the middle of the night, she could return the favor. She pushed the door open and stepped in, arms crossed in front of her chest.

Inside was a huge bedroom with peaked ceilings, thick carpet, and a king-size bed facing a bank of windows. Over the bed, a steady patter of rain fell on darkened skylights. Then her eyes landed on Roman, and every thought left her head.

He stood by his bed in nothing but boxer briefs. She'd seen him in his undershirts at George's, but nothing prepared her for this. Well-defined muscles flexed across his back as he turned to face her. His chest and arms were sculpted to perfection, the outline of his abs deepening with each breath he took.

The want in her cascaded like a waterfall, extinguishing every bit of frustration and leaving nothing but her fear. For the second time that night, tears sprung to life in her eyes.

He tossed down the T-shirt he'd been holding and stepped to her, putting one hand on each of her shoulders. His lips turned down in a frown as he searched her face. "Shay, what's wrong? What happened?"

She fought not to fall apart and forced herself to meet his gaze. "You happened. You tell me I'm your life and kiss me like that…" She took a deep breath, pushing back tears. "I just don't understand. You can barely look at me most days, and I know you've gone out of your way to avoid me. I'm not blind to the fact that I am clearly coming with a ton of baggage, and I'm so scared that it's too much." Her breath came out in a shaky exhale, and she looked down.

"Hey." He cupped her face, gently tipping it to look into his shimmering eyes. "I've been distant with you because I don't want to come in too fast and have you change your mind later. I don't want to be too much either, and it's killing me to know that if we start something now it'll be twisted up with what's happening with that psycho."

A tear escaped down her cheek, and she brushed it away. "I'm not going to change my mind. I thought about you every day I was gone. I thought I got you deported. I was sure you hated me, and I still couldn't let you go."

"If you only knew." The blue in his eyes glowed with a fire from within. "I can't bear the thought that when this situation with Kyle ends, you're going to realize you won't need me anymore."

Shay's breath hitched. "I'll need you. I want to be with you. I don't want to wait."

His face crumbled at her words, and his lips found hers. His warm hands wound their way around her back, underneath the shirt to bare skin, and pulled her close. She leaned into the embrace, forcing him to step back until they reached the bed and tumbled down.

****

Later, they lay side by side as their breathing slowly recovered. Roman clasped her hand in his and pulled it to him, kissing the back of her fingers before he let it rest on his bare chest. This was where she was meant to be. Overhead, the moon broke through the clouds.

Shay's stomach growled.

Roman rolled on his side and brushed a hair out of her face. "You didn't have time to eat before you tried to escape?"

"Something like that. Are you hungry?"

"Starving." He kissed the tip of her nose and swung out of bed to put on baggy gray sweatpants. "Let's go see what I have. I don't think it's much though."

Shay put the PJs he'd lent her back on and followed him to the kitchen. She opened cupboards while he checked the fridge.

He shut it a moment later and came up behind her, wrapping his arms around her and studying the near-bare cabinet over her head. "There's really nothing here. I can run over to Gisella's."

"No way. It's the middle of the night." Shay shooed him away. "Go sit. I've got this."

"Oh, you do, do you?" He smirked when she nodded and shooed him again.

The fridge was practically empty, but she'd found bread, peanut butter, and jelly in the cupboards. She made two sandwiches the way she liked, with toasted bread so the peanut butter melted.

She picked up the plates and found Roman starting a fire in the living room fireplace. Two glasses of amber liquid rested on the coffee table.

"Dinner is served." She held up the plates.

Roman put the screen over the crackling fire and joined her, taking his plate and sitting on the couch. "Tonight's special probably wouldn't have held a candle to this."

"Not all of us have a Michelin star," she shot back, taking a bite of her sandwich.

"Oh, you heard about that did you?"

"The old Roman wouldn't have stopped talking about it."

"Lucky for both of us, I've matured in my old age." He held out one of the glasses toward her and asked, "Nightcap?"

"Yes, please." She took a small sip, letting the smoky flavor take its time, burning as it went down her throat. "Oh, that's good."

"Lagavulin," he said. "I remember the company Christmas party just after you started at George's. You ordered one right after I did. I was stupid enough to think you were trying to catch my attention. But I don't think you even noticed me that night."

She smiled at the memory. "I noticed you. And I don't usually start my nights out with whisky, but I made an exception... Maybe to catch your attention."

"Funny, I don't remember you talking to me at that party." He rolled his glass in his hand swirling the amber liquid. "In fact, I distinctly remember every time I came near you, you had to suddenly use the bathroom, or get another drink, or talk to someone across the room."

"You must have conveniently forgotten, after my drink showed up so did your friend. The day bartender, Kaylie. Remember her?"

He winced. "Oh, her."

"Yeah, her. She draped herself around you and asked if you'd found her earring yet. One of the other waitresses saw me watching you two, and she took it upon herself to warn me that you had dated more than one of the staff members. Sometimes more than one at a time."

"So you turned me down every day for the next six months because of my bad reputation?"

"A very bad reputation," she emphasized. "But not just that. I was also working the shift that the waitress got fired for throwing a plate at your head."

"Amanda." Roman winced again.

Shay raised her eyebrows, point proven. "I heard a lot of stories about you and various *Amandas* from the other staff."

"All before I met you."

She cocked her head and paused her chewing.

He put up his hands in an act of surrender. "Seriously. Besides those two incidents from the first month I knew you, everything else was stories of my past. You never noticed I stopped dating?"

"Well, I didn't exactly think that. I thought you were seeing Gisella."

"Seriously? She told me that today, but she was drunk. I thought she must've misunderstood."

"Nope. I thought you stopped seeing the other women because things got serious with her."

"All this time, you thought I was with Gisella. And when I brought you to the island you thought…"

"She was your fiancée," she finished for him.

He laughed out loud. "How could you have never known? The guys in the kitchen were always giving me shit and trying to get me to set them up with her."

"You know I don't speak Spanish well enough to follow when you guys were talking fast. All I'd hear was her name and you yelling at someone. I thought you were defending her honor."

"In all fairness, I usually was defending her honor." He took another long drink.

"That's why I thought you stopped dating like a revolving door. And you being engaged explained why you've been so cold to me here."

"Trust me, there's nothing cold about me when it comes to you." He gave her a wicked look that sent heat all the way to her toes. He held up what was left of his sandwich. "You know, you really elevated this here. Toasting the bread is a game-changer. I wouldn't be surprised if a Michelin star is in your future." He finished the last of his sandwich in one bite and picked up both their empty plates.

"Shut up." She grinned, the whisky doing its work and warming her from the inside out. She picked up their glasses and followed him to the kitchen. "So, what was the special I missed out on tonight?"

"Dill poached salmon. You should know—you ordered it."

"I've been ordering whatever's on the special menu because I've liked them all. I don't know if you remember, but that dill salmon at George's was one of my favorites."

He rinsed the glasses and put them in a strainer to dry then toweled off his hands and stood in front of her, sighing. "I remember. You haven't noticed every special has been something I knew you loved?" He leaned in and kissed her jaw near her ear, whispering, "I really have lost my game."

The sensation of him so close sent a shock through her core, and her voice was rough as he pulled away. "You really haven't."

With a satisfied smile he backed away and checked the doors were locked, then double-checked that the security system was on. "Let's get some sleep."

She followed him back to his bedroom.

"Which side do you want?" he asked her.

"So, you'll be in here? Not secretly sleeping in the room next door?" She raised her eyebrows.

The corners of his mouth turned up, and he stepped toward her. "I'm not letting you out of my sight, and I'm not sleeping on any more floors." He scooped her up and tossed her onto the bed, climbing in behind her and pulling her close.

She turned her head toward him. "Roman, I know about Kyle hacking your system and releasing the guest information. I think I should leave in the morning. Maybe we can see if I can get FBI protection, but as long as I'm here, you're a target too."

"He didn't release shit." He nuzzled his face into the back of her neck, kissing her before his head dropped back down to the pillow. "Pete made a decoy. Kyle released a bunch of contact details for a donut chain paired with fake credit card info."

"Are you kidding?" A relieved laugh escaped Shay.

"I would guess he'll figure it out soon." He wound his fingers through Shay's hair.

Between her near delirium from being tired and the whisky, she blurted out, "If this gets to be too much with Kyle, I'll understand if you change your mind and want me to go at any point."

"If you leave, I leave. And I like it here." His voice rumbled through the dark. "Go to sleep."

Chapter 29

Kyle

The fucking slut.
Two a.m. Two-fucking-a.m. He'd been waiting for Shay in her room for hours now.

Kyle paced, his fists clenched in a struggle to not start smashing things. If she wasn't here by now, she wasn't coming back.

There was only one explanation—that stupid, fucking cook. She didn't even need him. Kyle could hire her the best chefs in the world if that's what she wanted. He stormed into the bathroom to splash water on his face and caught a glimpse of himself in her mirror. He was an absolute mess. His hair stood up from running his hands through it so much, eyes bloodshot and rimmed with dark circles, clothes rumpled. Unacceptable.

He splashed water on his face and tucked in his shirt. She wasn't here, but he was sure as hell going to find out where she was.

His laptop sat open on the desk. It had sent him an alert every time someone had gotten off the elevator even though none of the twenty-two times had been her. He slammed it shut and shoved it into his bag. Taking a deep breath, he opened the door to her room and strode down the hall to his own. Inside, he called the front

216

desk despite the late hour and extended his stay another night.

He had to regroup and re-plan. It was an island. He'd find her. Then he'd only have one choice left to make.

Which one of them he'd kill first.

Chapter 30

Roman

Roman woke with Shay still curled up beside him. He carefully slid his arm from underneath her, but she rolled with the movement, and her eyes drifted open. "You disappearing on me?"

"Only to go steal some food from Gisella's. Go back to sleep until you smell bacon." He kissed her forehead, pleased with the smile it brought even though her eyes had already closed.

He had to get it right. This wasn't a one-night stand. It wasn't just a fun time that he wasn't invested in. This was it. His girl.

He tugged on boots and keyed in the security code that would let him leave, but keep the system armed while he was gone. Cutting through the woods between their houses, he followed an unplanned path that had formed mostly from him and Pete going back and forth. They'd helped each other with projects at each house, had plenty of late-night beers, and Pete had once slept in Roman's guest room after a bad fight with Gisella. Roman knew her temper ran hot. He'd never deny a refugee shelter.

He jogged up the stairs to the deck and saw both Pete and Gisella through the window. The sliding door was unlocked, and he let himself in. It mirrored the same open concept of his but was furnished with a much more feminine touch.

"Hey, man. What brings you over here so early?" Pete said, taking a mouthful of eggs.

"I just came to rummage for supplies. My fridge is a little empty."

"Oh no, you're back home? Did something happen with Shay?" Gisella rapid-fired at him from where she stood near the stove.

"Yeah, it did." He grinned. "She's over there."

Gisella threw down the spatula in her hand. "Yes? That's fantastic. You confessed your love to her?" she exclaimed in Spanish.

"Something like that," Roman replied, a warmth spreading to his cheeks. He cleared his throat and switched to English for Pete's benefit. "Come on. Can I get some food to take over there?"

Gisella rushed to him, a ball of excited energy as she threw her arms around his neck. "*Mi amor* has found his *amor*. Of course. Take anything you want." Her words tumbled on top of each other as she gestured to the kitchen.

Roman extracted himself and opened the fridge, grabbing everything he needed to make omelets, plus milk for coffee. He barely got out without another hug from Gisella. She did get a promise from him to send Shay over when he left for work. The resort's weekly Grand Ball was later that night, and apparently Gisella had some ideas.

After trudging back through the woods, Roman kicked off his boots and went right to the kitchen. By the time Shay came down, he was sliding the second omelet onto a plate.

She looked relaxed, rumpled, and so beautiful standing in his kitchen wearing his favorite shirt.

She leaned over the plates. "Mmmm…that smells so good. Besides peanut butter sandwiches, I also make a mean cup of coffee."

"By all means." He pointed her in the direction of the coffee machine.

He turned off the security system and opened the French doors to the deck and the view of mist rising off the lake.

She brought two steaming mugs out and handed him one which he sipped, mildly surprised. "You know how I take my coffee?"

"What? You thought you were the only one paying attention?" She smirked, putting her mug down, and went in to get the plates.

When she came back, she set the plates on the table and walked to the railing to look over the edge. "What a peaceful place."

He finished drying off two of the chairs with an old towel and pulled them up to the table for them to sit. "Our dad worked here as the head gardener slash landscaper until he retired. The whole place closed shortly after."

"Oh, wow. Gisella said this place had special memories for her, but she didn't tell me anything beyond that."

"Yeah, she lived with her mom in Colombia almost the whole year, but in the summers, she would come stay here with us. It was incredible as a kid, basically like an unsupervised summer camp. My dad and I were a family on our own, but when Gisella was here it always felt more complete. He put his heart and soul into his work here. I can still see his touch all over this place."

"Did you and Gisella always plan to buy it?"

"No. That idea came a few years ago when he had a heart attack."

"I'm sorry," she said, putting down her cup. "That must have been hard. You guys sounded close."

"We were." It still didn't seem real that he was gone. "This is where he wanted his ashes scattered. When Gisella and I came, we saw how beautiful it still was despite being neglected. She called the owners that night. They were completely underwater, and she got it for a great deal. It took the past few years for her to get it the way she wanted it, and the timing with her retiring, then me leaving George's, was perfect."

"You couldn't have picked a better place. It reminds me a lot of where I live in Lake Placid."

"Do you think you'd ever consider moving back to Maine after this is all over, or does that feel like home now?" He looked down at his empty plate to avoid looking at her directly.

She pulled her bare feet up on the chair, knees tucked under her chin, hands cradling her coffee in front of her shins. She looked through the steam from her mug at him. "Nothing's felt like home since I met Kyle. I felt like I was in a prison until you brought me here. If I had my workshop, you may not be able to get rid of me when this is over."

"Hm," Roman said thoughtfully. He grabbed the plates. "Come on and get dressed. There's something I want to show you."

He pulled her clothes from last night out of the dryer and once she'd changed, he asked, "You up for a walk?"

"Sure."

They set out on a trail that overlooked the water before curving back into the woods. It ended in a clearing less than ten minutes later. In the middle, a barn rose up next to a stream.

"Watch your step." He pulled the door open, and they walked into the dusty, but open space. Sunlight poured through windows high overhead, landing on cluttered worktables and a few rusty machines. "This place was used as a workshop when I was a kid, but that was moved to the other side of the island long before my dad retired. I don't think anyone has set foot in here in at least ten years. I was a little surprised to find it still standing when I came out to look at it the other day."

He walked across the cluttered space. "It's already got electricity and a bathroom, but I was thinking we could clean it up, winterize it a little better, and maybe add some more windows over here." He pointed to the back wall, where another set of sliding doors currently were. "You know, so you'd have more light." He paused and slowly turned, realizing the immense amount of pressure he'd just put her under.

She hadn't moved from the doorway. His heart dropped as she glanced around, her gaze landing on everything from the exposed rafters to the creaky wooden floor. He should have at least waited until he could clear some of the old sawdust out before showing it to her. The longer she stayed silent the worse it got.

His mind was scrambling for a way to backtrack when she broke the silence. "You want me to move here to the island?"

Do or die. "I don't want to scare you by moving too fast. But yes, you have a place here, with me, if you want it."

The look on her face broke his heart. She seemed stunned, and took a deep breath, her forehead wrinkling, and eyebrows furrowed together. The gold flecks stood out as her eyes glistened. He'd pushed too hard. *Idiot.*

"I'm sorry. I knew this was too much to put on you with everything going on. I'm so sorry. Look, just forget I brought you here." He ran his hand over his hair. *If I ruined this already...*

"It's perfect," she said quietly, turning her gaze from the barn to him. "All of it. The barn. The island. You..."

He crossed the messy floor in quick strides and pulled her to him. Her soft lips melted against his, and relief cascaded through him like a waterfall. There was no doubt. He was hers.

When the kiss ended, Shay smiled up at him. "I'll take this over cheesy pick-up lines any day. You really have matured."

"I keep telling you." He trailed a finger down her cheek. "Plus, in case you haven't noticed, you're different for me."

"Yeah, I come with my own psycho stalker."

He grabbed her hand and steered her toward the door. "Not for much longer if I get my way."

"I don't know, Roman. How high on the FBI's priority list could this be? The whole spyware thing is bad, but they deal with so much worse."

He waited for a breath to answer, debating if there was any reason to keep avoiding telling her. But she deserved to know. "That's not all they're looking into."

He told her everything as they walked through the woods toward his house. Her frown deepened with every word until pure shock landed on her face when he told her about the girl from the hotel, Valerie.

"That's my fault." She stopped in the middle of the trail, fists balled at her sides.

"None of this is your fault," he affirmed facing her. "But if you want to blame anyone besides Kyle, blame me. I picked that hotel. It's on me." The painful thought had crossed his mind more than a few times since finding out the girl went missing.

"I knew he was dangerous, but I never imagined..." She cut herself off before finishing the thought and ran both hands through her hair. "He's just so in my head. I swear even now, for a second I thought I caught a whiff of his cologne." She took a deep breath, steadying herself, and Roman held out a hand for her to take.

"They're going to get him. There are two FBI agents on him twenty-four-seven until they get enough for an arrest. They know he's guilty. They aren't going to stop." He pulled her against his chest and wrapped his arms around her, wishing he could make her forget she'd ever had to waste a moment worrying about Kyle. He let her go when her breathing calmed, but she didn't stop scanning the forest around them as they walked until they caught the first glimpse of Gisella's house through the trees.

"Oh shit. I forgot that Gisella wanted you to go over before I left for work. She wants to talk to you about a dress for tonight's ball. You don't have to and if it's not your thing, we don't even have to go."

"No. It would be a good distraction. What time do you have to be at work?"

Roman gave a crooked smile. "About an hour ago."

Her eyes widened, and she swatted his arm. "Roman, go. I don't want to get you in trouble at this job, too."

"In trouble with who? I'm the boss." He laughed and took her hand before adjusting their course toward Gisella's. "When you're done here call the front desk, and they can send someone to pick you up."

"I'll find my way." Behind her smile, there was sadness that hadn't been there when they'd left his house. He hated that disclosing the information about Kyle was the most likely cause. He tilted her chin toward him with one finger and kissed her goodbye. "I'll pick you up for the ball at your room at eight?"

"Wow, full gentleman mode."

"Oh, you haven't seen anything yet." He pulled away, then leaned back down near her ear, and whispered, "Until tonight, *mi cielo*."

She let out a small gasp at his words, and he let his lips linger where her jaw met her ear before he backed away, pleased the sadness that had been in her eyes seemed at least temporarily erased.

Chapter 31

Kyle

Kyle stood perfectly still except for the slow vibration in his arms as they shook from rage. If he'd brought his gun, they'd both be dead. He'd followed them from Roman's house to the barn and now back to the sister's. Kyle had done his research, and he knew all about her. Supermodel turned real estate mogul, she'd chosen good investments and had quadrupled her money in only a few years. She might be an interesting conquest after this was wrapped up.

For now, he needed to focus on the task at hand. Roman may have just led him to the perfect place to act out the tableau that had formed in his head over the past twelve hours. Roman waited for Shay to go inside the model's house before leaving with a stupid grin on his face. Kyle debated following him home, but no, it would be too quick if he let his emotions overtake him. What he had planned was going to be better. He had to be patient. He pulled himself away to retrace his steps to the barn.

Arriving, he explored the inside and found a neglected workshop. He hadn't been close enough to see the inside before but it was all the better he hadn't rushed in with Roman just now. He would take his time making up for the disappointment of last night. He scoured the barn and collected things that would come in useful—a couple of chairs, some rope, a hammer, and a chisel. He envisioned the night over and over and chose carefully where he wanted the chairs to face before nailing two of them to the ground. He took the time to scout the area and found an overgrown dirt road that led back to one of the paved paths. It would be bumpy, but it looked drivable. When he was finished, he made a trip to his hotel room, careful to keep his baseball cap and sunglasses on until he reached the safety of his room.

He gathered the last of the supplies he'd need and returned to the barn. He set his backpack on the main workbench and pulled out his computer along with a cellphone jammer. Satisfied that everything was ready, he sank into one of the chairs and flicked open the screen of his phone to text Jace.

—*Missing you*—

They had a simple code. Anytime Kyle reached out, he wanted an update. His phone was linked to a fake account, and texts from him would come from a Ms. Katie Ashbury. Jace never took long to answer.

—*Still home sick but otherwise all good. I'll hit you up tomorrow.*—

Good. Still no problems on that end. Kyle checked the cameras at his house and saw the FBI detail was still out front. He flipped shut his laptop and watched the sun sink away as he rolled over his plans for the night in his mind. After he enjoyed some time alone with Shay, he'd find a way to ambush Roman tomorrow. Once he had them both at the barn the fun could really start.

He left and started a slow jog back to the hotel.

There was plenty of time to shower and change into the shirt he'd stolen from the resorts uniform closet, but he didn't want to rush. This was going to be a big night.

Chapter 32

Shay

After their trip to the barn, Roman's kiss lingered on Shay's lips as she walked up the stairs to Gisella's deck.

Gisella opened the door. "Oh, I wish Roman wasn't my brother because I would love to hear the details of whatever happened between you two to make you glow like that."

"It's not like that." Shay touched her cheeks knowing they just got redder as Gisella cut her off.

"Bup bup bup, no details, please." She held up one finger.

Shay rolled her eyes, and Gisella pulled her inside.

"Come with me. I have some things for you to try on."

"Gisella, unless you've had a period in your life where you were five inches shorter and at least four sizes bigger, I don't stand a chance of fitting into your clothes."

"Just come." She led Shay down a hall that opened into a master suite with an entire dressing room instead of a closet. Gisella went to a rack that held five dresses and pulled one off. "These, I got for you. They arrived yesterday." She held up the first dress.

It was an inky black sleeveless number that looked

more expensive than Shay's whole wardrobe. "It's gorgeous! Where did you get it?" She reached out and let the material slide through her fingers.

"Some designers I know." Gisella shrugged. "Try it on."

Shay did try it on, and the other four. Each one would easily be the most gorgeous thing she'd ever worn. Gisella was set on a short, red one that hugged all her curves, but Shay was in love with the black one until she tried on the last. It was baby blue with spaghetti straps and a slit from floor to upper thigh that you didn't see until she moved. The fabric cascaded around her like it was made of liquid. Centered in the middle of the chest was a beautifully cut quarter-sized crystal that caught every flicker of light.

When Shay first stepped out from behind the clothing rack wearing it, Gisella said nothing. Instead, she stepped back with fingers tented in front of her smile, eyes wide, and just nodded. Her expression mirrored Shay's thoughts.

"It's perfect." Gisella finally stepped toward where Shay stood in front of the mirror and twisted Shay's long hair up and off her shoulders.

"I never want to take it off." Shay couldn't stop staring at herself.

"Oh, you shouldn't. This dress was made for you." Gisella started pulling out boxes. "Now we need the shoes."

They settled a pair of heels with thin bands of crystals for straps. "Thank you so much, Gisella."

"Of course." She waved her away. "Take it all off for now, and I'll have it pressed and sent to your room. Tonight's going to be so much fun."

Shay walked back to the hotel, finally shaking the feeling she was being watched for the first time that day. She got a coffee and found a quiet spot in a porch swing with an attached footrest. The gentle rocking and warm breeze lulled her to sleep within minutes.

An hour later, the scent of the peppery cologne that had been haunting her the past few days yanked her from her dreams. She sprang out of the chair and whipped her head around. No one was near her. She let out a breath and leaned against the railing, then froze. Below, a man had just passed by. Same build as Kyle, same swagger. Stumbling, she started to follow him, skirting furniture while trying to keep her eyes on him.

Turn. Turn! she willed, wanting to see his face and be sure she was just being paranoid. She caught his profile as he entered the hotel, and Shay took off running. It was him. He had sunglasses and a hat, but it was him.

She practically flew to Manuel's desk.

"Good morning, Ms. Cole." If he was surprised she'd come in sprinting, he hid it well.

"I need Pete, now."

"Of course." He picked up his radio and brought it to his mouth. "Pete. What's your location?"

The scratchy reply was almost immediate. "En route to the hotel. Crossing the lawn now."

Shay ran back toward the front door while Manuel replied, "Ms. Cole is on her way to meet you."

Her feet thundered down the path until she met his cart.

"What happened?" His eyes lasered in on hers.

"He's here." She gasped for breath. "I saw him."

"Where?" He changed channels on his radio and

held it ready for her response.

"Going into the hotel through the courtyard entrance."

He pushed the talk button on his radio. "Code red. All eyes out for Kyle Matthews. He was just seen entering through the courtyard entrance." He took his finger off the button and asked Shay, "What was he wearing?"

"Gray hoodie and sunglasses." Her heartbeat pounded in her ears.

"Gray hoodie, sunglasses. Detain immediately." He looked at her. "Get in."

She ran to the passenger side, and he made a U-turn, aiming the golfcart toward a path she'd never been down.

"Where are we going?"

"The security command center. Until we find him, you'll be safe there."

A few minutes later, they arrived at a nondescript building nestled well off the main path. After typing out a code on a keypad, Pete led her into a dim room with a whole wall of nothing but monitors. The two security staff manning them stood when Pete walked in. "Shay, this is Tom and Julio. Help them find where you last saw Kyle so we can track where he went."

Pete opened another door to a more well-lit room and disappeared through it. Tom found the camera angle that showed the swing Shay had been in but when he pulled up the footage, an older man reading a paper was in the seat she should have been occupying. They rewound twenty minutes, still the man, then thirty minutes, to a now vacant chair.

"Something's not right," she said as they went back

farther and farther with no sign of her. Julio cued the tape back up to present and began rewinding frame by frame. Suddenly, from one frame to the next, the whole scene changed, different people, lighting, flowers blowing in one were still in the next.

Julio rolled his chair over to a desktop computer and started clicking through screens of scrolling text as Pete came back in with his phone pressed to his ear. "We have a problem here, boss," Julio said to him, now clicking keys at a furious rate.

"What?" Pete frowned.

"Our live feeds are fine, but as soon as we try to rewind, it's looping back to footage from four days ago."

Pete's frown deepened, and he responded to someone on the phone, "You're sure he's still in his house? We just found that he's tampering with our security footage. That would be great, thanks."

He hung up and let out a big exhale. "That was Agent Hiller. He says Kyle hasn't moved from his house. Kyle must have figured out how to hack in remotely."

"No. I saw him, Pete," Shay said. "Why would he be messing with the security footage if he wasn't here?"

"My best guess is he's planning on being here. Us finding this gives us a leg up though. We can find the backdoor he got in through and the second they tell us he leaves that house, we can shut it, hopefully without him noticing."

"I was sure it was him." She had been half asleep at the time, and whoever was wearing the same cologne had been throwing her off for days. "It was a quick look, and there were sunglasses, but I really thought it was him."

"Hey, it's okay. If you hadn't sounded the alarm, we wouldn't have found this little trap he set." Pete put an arm around her and gave her a squeeze. Outside there was a roar of an engine. Pete stiffened as the front door slammed open. "Oh shit."

"Where is he?" Roman stormed towards the monitors after looking Shay over.

"It was a false alarm," Pete said.

Shay quickly added, "I'm sorry. It was my mistake. I only got a glimpse, and someone here's wearing his cologne. I think it's messing with me more than I thought."

"Yeah, well, her mistake found a huge security breach so I'd call this a win," Pete told Roman.

"And you're sure he's not here?" Roman looked to Pete for reassurance.

"Hiller just confirmed he's still in his house," Pete replied. "I'm going to double security going forward though. If he's messing with our security cameras, he may be getting close to making his move."

"I wish he would," Roman said, some of the fire in his eyes dulling. He turned to Shay. "You're okay?"

"I'm fine, just embarrassed for overreacting."

"Better to overreact than underreact," Julio called, without taking his eyes off the monitor.

"See," Pete said, pointing at Julio.

"Come on. I'll take you back." Roman led her to where he'd left the four-wheeler running, parked as close to the door as it could be without going through.

She got on behind him and, for the second time in twenty-four hours, rested her cheek on his back letting the warmth and rhythm of his breathing comfort her as they went back through the side trails, skirting most of the guests. Roman walked her all the way to her room, and she felt increasingly guilty that she'd once again interrupted his day and created more drama that had him worried.

"I'm sorry, again." She opened the door to her room and he came in, poking his head into the bathroom and around the corner to the bedroom.

"Don't be sorry." He held each of her shoulders. "I'm on edge, too. This will end, and we'll move on." His voice was reassuring as he tucked her head under his chin.

She clasped her hands behind his sturdy back and let the solidness of him hold her up.

"Do you still want to go tonight?"

"Even if I didn't, it would be a crime to waste the dress Gisella got me."

"Something to look forward to then." He kissed her then backed away. "See you tonight."

Shay spent the rest of the afternoon working on a couple half-finished sketches of design ideas, but her mind kept returning to the nagging feeling of insecurity that had been present since the morning. She'd rationalized it up and down: Kyle was in Portland; he had FBI agents watching him; it would make him happy knowing how much he was in her head. Nothing helped calm her unease, so when she pulled on the dress, she tucked the small pocketknife that she kept in her purse into the base of the dress's built-in bra.

Feeling a little better, she smiled at the full-length mirror. Shay didn't use makeup on a daily basis besides some mascara and lip gloss, but luckily, she'd packed the basics when she thought she was going to Alex's goodbye party. Her hair was mostly pinned-up, leaving a few strands curled down here and there. Slipping on the shoes completed the look, and she smiled at her reflection, trying to remember if Roman had ever seen her in so much as a skirt. When he knocked at eight, butterflies fluttered to life in the pit of her stomach as she opened the door.

The suit he wore was tailored to fit him perfectly, and the smell of his aftershave was mouthwatering. His blue eyes sparkled as he looked her over head to toe, letting out a low whistle. He stood completely still with eyes locked on Shay's then shook his head. It was beyond gratifying to be the reason he looked like a deer caught in headlights. She reached back to the dresser to pick up her room key and tucked it into the small clutch Gisella had lent her. The dress slid over her skin like oil as she walked out the door.

Roman stood frozen in place, staring but not saying a word.

"Ready?" She raised her eyebrows when he didn't move after she stepped into the hallway and shut the door.

"I honestly don't know." He ran a hand over his head. "You look...I don't know. You look...wow," he stammered out.

She laughed. "I warned you about the dress."

"You look incredible." He still didn't move.

She reached out and took his hand to pull him forward toward the elevator.

Chapter 33

Roman

Roman let her lead him toward the elevator, still too taken to speak. Shay was beautiful after a long day of waitressing, with messy hair and a stained shirt. This was something else entirely. *Breathtaking.*

The elevator opened to a sea of elegantly dressed guests filling the Great Hall. Waiters circled the room with trays of champagne and hors d'oeuvres. Couples were drawn to the space being used for a dance floor as a live band played an upbeat song.

A bar stretched along one wall, and Gisella stood at its end, talking to an older couple. She glanced over at them and excused herself to glide across the room in her wrap-around, navy blue gown.

"You look beautiful." She kissed Shay on each cheek before turning to Roman, smiling. "And you look speechless."

"Well…I don't think…you know," he mumbled.

"Oh my God. You are speechless." She clapped her hands together, laughing as a waiter approached with a tray of champagne. Gisella took a glass and pressed in into Roman's hand. "Drink up. Boy, are you in trouble." She reached for two more for herself and Shay.

Gisella stayed close to Shay and pointed out

different couples, giving her a who's who of the current guests while Roman pounded the first glass of champagne and got a second. Once the alcohol steadied his nerves, he joined the conversation.

A steady stream of guests approached, mainly interested in praising the resort or the food. Nothing distracted him enough to keep his gaze off Shay for long.

When she placed her empty glass on a passing waiter's tray, Roman leaned down to her. "Dance with me."

She nodded and took the hand he offered.

Even with heels, she was a few inches shorter than him, and she looked up as he put one hand solidly on her back, the other intertwining her fingers with his. He pulled her fingertips toward him, kissing the back of her hand gently before he led her smoothly around the dancefloor, expertly guiding them between other couples.

When the song ended and the music switched to a slow song, he didn't miss a beat and pulled her closer.

"How'd you learn to dance so well?" she asked as he caught his breath.

"It was Gisella's pet project one summer. I didn't think boys needed to learn, but she convinced me it would impress girls."

"She was right."

"Tell that to the thirteen-year-olds who thought I was insane when I tried to waltz with them at my first school dance."

"They didn't know what they were missing."

"Glad you think so because I need to keep you interested. You've caught the eye of every guy in this room." He pulled her a little closer.

"Really? Which ones in particular?" She glanced around, then looked at him out of the corner of her eye.

He laughed. "Oh, that's how it's going to be?"

"I don't know if you remember…but I used to get a marriage proposal every few days from you. I haven't gotten even one in the week I've been here."

"There's a good reason for that."

"You're scared away by the small detail of me having a homicidal maniac stalker who's making me lose my mind?" She raised her eyebrows.

"Hardly. Maybe I've refined my flirting technique." He slowed their dance to a stop and used his hand to tilt her head up so she looked into his eyes. "Or maybe I decided that the next time I propose to you, I'll be on one knee and expecting an answer."

He slid his hand from her chin, down her arm, and over the goosebumps that had broken out there. Shay opened her mouth but paused without saying anything. If she did have a response in mind, Roman didn't get to hear it. They were interrupted by the sous chef.

"Pardon me." Ricky glanced at Shay, then back to Roman. "I'm so sorry, Chef, but there's a call for you."

Roman didn't take his eyes from Shay. "Take a message."

"It's the CDC."

"What?" His head snapped toward Ricky.

In a low voice, the sous chef frantically relayed the message. "There's a Listeria outbreak at one of the farms that supply our produce distributor. They need a guest list from last week through today. Anyone who ate here needs to be contacted."

Roman let go of Shay, cursing in Spanish under his

breath. He turned to her. "I'm sorry."

"It's okay. Go. That sounds bad."

"It's really bad." *Like career ending.*

The sous chef had left to deliver the same news to Gisella, and both walked quickly back toward Roman. A forced smile was plastered on Gisella's face as she nodded to the guests she passed.

"Come on. Let's figure out what has to be done," she said to Roman, then to Shay, "Tell Pete what happened when Mr. Fashionably-late graces the party with his presence."

"Of course." Shay's gaze swung to Roman one last time.

"Stay and enjoy. I'll be back as soon as I can," he promised.

"Don't worry about it. I'll save a dance for you."

"You better save all of them for me." He grinned, memorizing exactly how she looked before he turned to deal with something much worse than anything Kyle could have thrown at them.

****

Roman could hear the frustration in his own voice by the time he got through to a human at the CDC's after-hours line. "No. Someone called *us.* They left this number. No. I don't have their name. They said it was about a Listeria outbreak."

"Well, I'll patch you through to the emergency office, but I can tell you from the active list of outbreaks, we don't have any Listeria affecting Maine. Hold, please."

"I don't like this," Roman said to Gisella across his desk. "Can you call Pete and have him stay with Shay till we get back up there?" He cursed himself internally for not thinking of it sooner.

Gisella nodded and turned around, pulling a cell phone from her purse.

A man's gruff voice came through the speakerphone on Roman's desk. "How can I help you?"

"This is Chef Roman Garcia from The Sanctuary Resort in Maine. Did someone from your office contact us about a Listeria outbreak?"

"If they did, it was a mistake. Do you know—"

Roman dropped the phone, his heart pounding with fear.

Gisella's eyes flicked to him, panic mirrored on her face. "Pete's not answering."

Roman took off running up the side stairs and through Sueno's kitchen. He burst into the Great Hall, scanning the crowd. There was no commotion. No struggle anywhere he could see, but also no Shay. In his pocket, his phone vibrated, and he clicked on the blocked number. "Hello."

"Roman Garcia?"

Roman's breath hitched. "Agent Hiller."

"I've been trying to reach Sergeant Moss. Matthews used a body double to pose as him for the past few days. We traced the numbers that have been texting with the fake Kyle. One is pinging from a cell tower near you."

Roman's words tumbled out. "Both Pete Moss and Shay Cole are currently missing." *Better to overreact.*

"I'm with a team on my way to you, and we've alerted local authorities. You need to take every precaution you can, immediately."

"Understood." Roman clicked off the call and headed straight for the receptionist at the front desk.

"I need a radio. Now."

The girl jumped at his command and fumbled as she handed it over.

He flipped to the security channel and held it to his mouth. "Code red." He took a deep breath. After the situation earlier, Pete had provided the entire team with digital photos of Kyle so they would all be ready to keep an eye out.

He held down the talk button. "Kyle Matthews is on the property and needs to be found." Looking across the room, he made eye contact with one of the plain-clothed security staff members circulating the ball. "Tony, check the vault for Pete. Now."

Tony brought his wrist to his mouth where he had a hidden radio mic in the cuff. "Copy."

Roman pressed the talk button again and gave the next commands. "The FBI and local police will be arriving shortly. I want them met and briefed. Give them access to anything they need. Everyone else, search the grounds for Kyle."

A round of "copies" came through, signaling each of the staff had heard the message as Roman spotted Manuel. His eyes searched the room for Shay while he strode toward the concierge.

Gisella fell into step with him halfway there.

He continued scanning the crowd. "I have them looking for Pete."

Gisella nodded. "I'll check upstairs. Maybe Shay went to her room."

Roman pulled out his key card and handed it to her, motioning for another one of the plain-clothes guards to come over. "Nick, go with Gisella. Don't leave her side until we find Kyle."

"Yes, sir." The man raced to keep up as Gisella took off for the elevator.

Roman reached the small cluster of guests surrounding Manuel and interrupted the conversation. He was well past caring about keeping a calm façade. "Manuel—"

"Ah, hello, Romeo." Manuel's charming smile faded as soon as he took in Roman's face.

"Have you seen Shay?"

"She got your message to meet you in the café courtyard."

Bile churned in Roman's stomach. "How long ago?"

"Maybe twenty minutes. Why? What is it?"

Roman didn't answer. He took off at a full sprint, radio at his mouth. "Shut down the dock. Get eyes on every side of this island and make sure no one leaves. Who's monitoring the cameras?"

"Tom, here. What do you need?"

"Cue up the footage of the café courtyard going back half an hour. Tell me if you see Shay on it."

Roman ran out the front door and took the porch steps two at a time, reaching the courtyard within seconds. It was empty, like he expected, but losing that last glimmer of hope hit like a gut punch, and he struggled to take a full breath. He paced, tugged his tie loose, and yanked off his jacket, balling it up and flinging it at a chair.

"Fuck!" The helpless word exploded from him while he waited for Tom to tell him which direction to run in.

He jammed his hands into his pants pocket and touched the little plastic box that contained a now-melted chocolate rose. He'd planned on giving it to Shay when he picked her up at her room earlier that night. He'd forgotten it, along with his own name, when she opened the door. The memory came with an overwhelming tightness in his chest, reminiscent of when she disappeared months ago. He stopped short of punching the stone wall when Tom's voice brought his attention back to the radio.

"At nine-ten, the video shows Shay walking into the courtyard. A man approaches her from behind. She collapses, and he carries her to a golf cart on the east-bound path."

"Where do they go?" Roman was already running toward the vehicle storage.

"They continue east to the woods, then break off toward the residences."

The residences. Roman and Gisella's homes. "Get men there, now," Roman barked.

"Already on their way." Tom signed off.

It had been just over half an hour since he took her. A half-hour head start. A half-hour where he could be doing anything. Roman's thoughts tumbled over one another as he drove the four-wheeler across the lawn, plunging into the darkness as the trees filtered out the moonlight.

He flicked on the headlights and flew down the main path, tires screeching as he took the turn to his and Gisella's houses. This was the last place Tom had seen Shay on the video. The cameras only monitored guest areas, but nothing else was over here for Kyle to take Shay to.

Then it hit him...*the barn.* Shay had thought she imagined smelling Kyle's cologne earlier. What if she hadn't imagined it? He slammed on the brakes and pulled out his radio.

"Tom. Come in."

No answer. He tried again. Still no answer. Roman switched channels and was met with static. He dug out his phone. No bars.

There were rarely service issues on the island. Kyle must be using a jammer, and he must be close. Roman didn't debate the cost of wasting time to backtrack out of range of the jammer and call for help. He had to get to Shay.

He reversed the four-wheeler, remembering the general area of the driveway that wound to the barn. It was a painstakingly slow search to find the overgrown entrance. He was a quarter-mile down its bumpy path when he caught the first flicker of light through the trees and knew he was right. For a split second, he debated going for the element of surprise. It would take too much time. Time that would delay interrupting whatever was going on in the barn. He tore around the last bend in the driveway, engine screaming.

Chapter 34

Shay

"There's my sleeping beauty." The soft-spoken words cut through the fog in Shay's head, and her eyelids lifted, blinking away the film that blanketed her eyes. Kyle's image came into focus in front of her. Shay tried to stand, but a wrenching pain in both her shoulders pulled her back down to the chair she was tied to, hands secured tightly behind her back.

"Let me go." The words came slowly, her tongue thick from whatever he'd drugged her with.

"But you just got here. Come on, let's catch up a little." Kyle pulled off a jacket with the resort's logo on it, exposing a white button-up shirt underneath. Dried blood stained a good portion of the front of it. He followed her gaze, glanced down, and began to unbutton the shirt. "Sorry. I didn't have time to clean up, but don't worry. It's not my blood."

She stayed silent, keeping her eyes on the floor, terrified to ask.

"Some director of security your boyfriend has here. I've never killed a man before, and I have to say it was a little disappointing. I've had plenty of women put up a better fight." Kyle pulled off the stained shirt. "I thought he'd be at the ball already, and he almost got the jump on me when we crossed paths. Luckily, I saw him first, and a gunshot wound to the head is pretty much a trump card."

She tried to keep her face a mask and told herself he was bluffing until she remembered Gisella being mad because Pete was late. *Oh, God. Pete.* She bit the inside of her lip and kept her eyes trained on a rake against the far wall.

"I planned on looking much sharper for our night together, but man, I see now I would have been underdressed anyway." He tossed his ruined shirt aside, leaving just a white tank top stretched across his muscular chest. "You really look spectacular." He bent down in front of her and gently pushed back a lock of hair that had fallen into her face. He trailed a finger down her cheek, searching her eyes with his. "What is it about you that makes me want you so bad?"

She gritted her teeth. "If I knew, I'd change it."

A wide smile showed all his teeth, and he slipped into a southern accent. "Now don't be like that, darlin'."

Her blood ran cold, and tears of terror sprung to her eyes. *Toby.*

A beep sounded from his open laptop, set up on a workbench nearby. He frowned and went over to look, letting out a surprised laugh. "Well, well, looks like company is coming earlier than expected."

Shay tried loosening her hands, but it only caused the rough rope to bite into her wrists.

He shook his head and walked back to her. "And I thought I was being paranoid by setting up a motion-triggered camera, but maybe the dishwasher is smarter than he looks." He cocked an eyebrow. "Then again, he's alone, so maybe not."

"He's smarter than you are."

"I very much doubt that." Kyle crossed to a bag in the corner and pulled out a handgun. "Either way, this should tip things in my favor."

"No," she yelled, trying to stand.

He stared at her. "You love him."

She didn't answer, and he squatted right in front of her, his face inches from hers. "You do, don't you?"

She turned to avoid the intensity of his gaze.

He grabbed her face to turn it back to him. "I hope you do. That will make this all the more entertaining." Any trace of sadness or jealousy was gone in a blink and replaced with cold anger as he tightened his grip on her and ground his lips against hers. She bit him. He pulled back and swung his arm up in one motion, hitting her across the face with the butt of the gun.

Her head rocked back, and her cheek exploded with white-hot pain, but she kept her composure, not wanting to give him any satisfaction. She took a deep breath and spat the taste of his blood from her mouth.

"Ohhh, I like a girl who can take a little pain." He tucked the gun in the back of his pants and pulled out a hunting knife from the side pocket of his bag. He snaked himself behind her, wrapped one arm tightly around her neck, and pressed the tip of the blade under her chin as the engine roared closer. "I was hoping we could enjoy ourselves alone, but if we're going to have an audience, I'll make sure to put on a good show." He squeezed her tighter. Suddenly it was hard to take a full breath.

The door flung open. Roman stepped inside, his focus landing on Shay first. His gaze flicked from her swollen cheek to her terrified eyes, then zeroed in on

Kyle. "Let her go."

"I don't think you're in any position to make requests," Kyle said. "Tell me, are you still going to want her if this pretty face is all cut up?" He slid the tip of the blade across her cheek.

Roman stepped forward, and Kyle threw the knife down to the floorboards where it stood up straight, stuck in the wood. In one fluid motion, he pulled out the gun with his other hand and pointed it at Shay's head, halting Roman.

Kyle gestured to an empty chair next to a workbench. "Why don't you have a seat?"

Roman glanced at the gun, then moved to the chair.

"Good boy. Put your hands behind your back," Kyle commanded.

Shay locked eyes with Roman. "Don't do it. If he kills me, it's over for him. He's not going to, yet."

Kyle let go of Shay and stepped between her and Roman. "You know, she's right. Of course, just because I'm not going to kill her until I'm thoroughly tired of her doesn't mean I won't hurt her in the meantime. So, maybe I shoot her somewhere that won't kill her?" He raised the gun to point at her knee, her stomach, and her arm, each in turn. He looked her up and down, then swung the gun back up to her head before meeting Roman's eyes. "Or maybe I realized you found us so quickly that others are sure to follow, and I should cut my losses and go."

Roman stayed still, saying nothing as Kyle pulled a zip tie out of his bag. He slipped it around Roman's wrists, pulled it tight, and leaned in toward Roman's ear. "No, I don't think we need to rush. As you said earlier, no one knows about this place, and if you'd been with anyone, they would've shown up by now. Plus, I have radio and cell service blocked for a mile in each direction, so I doubt you called anyone."

Roman swung his head back trying to connect with Kyle's face, but he pulled away. "Uh uh uh. Too slow." Kyle smiled as he stood, and with no warning, twisted, throwing a punch that made full contact with Roman's face.

Shay screamed, but Roman rolled his head back to midline and stared up at Kyle, one eye already swelling.

Kyle let out a humorless laugh. "Oh, tough guy. That's what you like, Shay? He's a tough guy?" He landed another punch. "He has something you think I can't give you?" He punched again.

"Stop! Please stop!" Shay begged. "I'll do whatever you want."

With fire in his eyes, Roman spat, "Shay, no."

Kyle landed one more hit, then turned his attention away from Roman and onto Shay with a wild anger in his eyes. "Oh, I know you're going to do whatever I want. And right now I want you to fucking scream." Kyle put the gun on a high shelf and stooped next to Shay, yanking the knife free from the floorboards.

When he circled behind her, she expected to feel the blade cut her at any moment, but instead, there was a sharp tug to both wrists as he sliced through the rope. She pulled her hands forward and rubbed her wrists. Both shoulders burned from being stretched backward for so long.

Behind her, Kyle said, "Go, Shay. You want to go, right? There's the door."

She stayed where she was. It had to be a trick…but her hands were free, and she still had the knife hidden in her dress. Compared to his dagger, it was a toothpick, and any damage it could inflict on Kyle would be a temporary distraction at best. His hands were in her hair, gently pulling out the pins that held it up off her shoulders. He dropped each one to the floor, then combed his fingers through her curls. "As soft as I imagined." He twisted the hair around his fist in one quick motion and jerked her head back, causing her to let out another yell. "Stand up." He didn't give her a chance before dragging her by her hair to the workbench. He shoved her forward hard and pushed her face down onto the table.

"You piece of shit! Get your hands off her." Roman thrashed in the chair, straining against the restraints but getting nowhere since it was nailed to the floor.

Shay struggled, trying to free her arms but Kyle's hands were everywhere. "Keep fighting. It's only going to make it better for me." He swept her hair aside and kissed her neck.

Her hand found the end of a dowel, and she let out a moan of pleasure, hoping to throw him off guard. As soon as she did, he loosened his grip to turn and look at Roman. She took advantage and swept her arm, connecting the wood with the side of his head. She shoved back as he fell to the side.

"Run, Shay," Roman commanded.

She ran, but not to leave like he wanted. Instead, she ran to him, seeing his battered face for the first time up close.

"Go," he yelled, turning his head from her as she gently touched his bruised cheek with one hand.

She wrapped her other arm around him and pressed

the pocketknife into his palm.

Kyle regained his footing and barreled toward them as Roman pleaded with Shay one more time. "Go."

Rough hands yanked her off Roman and flung her to the ground behind him. "She puts up a better fight than you."

"Untie me and see what kind of fight I put up," Roman growled, rage written across his face.

"Maybe later." Kyle turned back to where Shay struggled to get up. He knelt and pushed her back down, pinning her with his body.

With her eyes squeezed shut, her fingernails dug into the skin of his neck as she tried to force him away. Then, his crushing weight was gone.

She pushed her feet into the wood floor, propelling herself backward before standing up and running for the shelf with the gun. Her knife may not be able to do too much damage to Kyle, but Roman could. That was what she was banking on when she'd slipped it to him seconds ago.

The gun was too high up for her to reach. She turned her attention to where Roman had slammed Kyle into a wall. After the initial shock wore off, Kyle fought back, but the anger that had built in Roman was explosive. Kyle only got in a few hits before Roman had him on the ground, landing blow after blow.

Shay scanned the room for anything that would help her reach the gun. Roman would kill Kyle if nothing stopped him. Before she had to decide if she should try, the door flew open and Agent Hiller stormed in, gun drawn and barking commands to the team behind him. It took two of them to pull Roman off Kyle.

Shay crashed into him. He winced and let out a grunt but pulled her against him and held her tight.

Kyle smirked when an agent yanked him to his feet, reading him his rights. He spat blood to the floor and looked at Roman. "Just wait until my lawyer gets a hold of this. You'll have a battery charge. You'll do time for this, dishwasher."

Agent Hiller put the cuffs on him. "You're gonna want to exercise your right to remain silent. You don't currently have representation, but you'll be provided with a public defender. I advise consulting with them before saying anything further."

"No, dipshit. My representation is Shawn Collaway. Of Collaway, Gallo, and Smith. You may have heard of them," he said, naming one of the most prestigious law firms on the East Coast.

"I sincerely doubt that. It seems daddy controls your purse strings, and I personally spoke with your father today. Very reasonable guy. Smart, too. He's decided to cut you off."

"Impossible. He wouldn't give a shit about whatever bullshit stalking story you've been wasting your time on."

"That could very well be true," Agent Hiller said. "But I didn't even bother telling him about this whole mess you've created." He gestured to where Shay held tightly onto Roman. "No, I led with the multiple girls you murdered. He was actually most cooperative after I showed him the footage we found, from a ice cream shop of all places, when you had the girl from the Hampstead drugged in the front seat of your car. Seems you decided to stop for a snack before you raped and murdered her. After that, he granted us access to search your townhouse and collect whatever DNA we need. The senator had no trouble believing you were capable of murder. He even seemed to take a great deal of the responsibility on himself for bailing you out of lesser evils in the past."

Kyle's face blanched. "You're full of shit."

"We're about to go find out, aren't we?" Agent Hiller let another agent take over to read him his charges and his rights.

"Kyle Matthews, you are under arrest for…"

The list of charges was so long that when officers led him away, they were still listing offenses.

"We have a medical team working on the other victim. We'll take you over to them so they can check you both out," Agent Hiller said.

"Other victim?" Roman asked.

"Your head of security, Pete Moss, sustained a gunshot wound, but it's not life-threatening."

"Kyle said he shot him in the head," Shay piped up, unsure how that could not be life-threatening.

"It ricocheted off a steel plate. He's being treated for a concussion and ruptured eardrum but will be fine." Agent Hiller added, "He pointed us in this direction, and we were able to use satellite images to find this structure."

"I guess that's the last time I make fun of him for being hardheaded," Roman said as the two of them walked out to sit in a waiting golf cart. Remaining in the barn was not an option they would consider.

"He has a plate in his head?" Shay asked. In front of her, an officer handcuffed Kyle. He was still hurling threats of lawyers as he was led to another cart.

"He has a bullet lodged in an inoperable part of his

brain from his special forces days. It's why they made him retire."

An agent came up to them and said, "I'm going to take you to the medics."

They didn't argue, and he drove them back down the driveway. Every bump brough a new ache or pain in her battered body as the surrealness of the night started to fade and reality set in. Turning onto the paved path was a relief, and it was only a few more minutes before they came upon a group of people surrounding one of the hotel's two medical transport vehicles. Pete lay on the gurney.

"Oh my God!" Shay jumped out before they had fully stopped when she saw the bandage on his head was soaked through with blood.

"It looks worse than it is. I'm a bleeder." Pete propped himself up on the gurney to look at Shay. "They're making me go to the hospital. Totally unnecessary."

"You were shot in the head," Shay stated.

"I've had worse." Pete blew it off. "But please tell Gisella I'm suffering incredibly and being very tough and manly the whole time."

Roman declined. "Gisella catches me lying, and she'll have me suffering incredibly. So, no thanks."

"Fine. But she's probably going to do worse to me for standing her up tonight. I can hear it now: *It was barely a graze, pendejo*," he said, in a perfect Gisella accent.

"I think we're about to find out," Roman said as Gisella pulled up in the second medical truck.

A stream of angry Spanish switched to English as she came closer. "You fool! Getting shot in the head again." She climbed in the back of the truck next to him, gently cradling his face as she inspected him despite her angry words. "You are the luckiest guy in the world."

"Aw, babe, I knew that the second you agreed to marry me."

"You idiot," she said, tears of relief spilling from her eyes as she gently kissed him while the medics closed the doors.

Roman and Shay passed their field exams, but they were warned that they would be sore and to watch for signs of a concussion as another medic dropped them off at Roman's house.

As they stepped inside, Roman turned exhausted eyes on her. "Go on upstairs. I'm going to reset the alarm system and call the hotel to make sure things are taken care of."

She nodded and went to his room, finding a soft button-up shirt she could pull on without straining her sore shoulders. Her dress was beyond saving, but she still carefully hung it up before getting into a hot shower.

The water worked magic on her, starting to ease the tension, and she let the glass steam up without moving. The door opened, and Roman stepped in. He joined her under the hot stream and gently pulled her into his embrace.

She gasped at his muscular body fully visible in the light. He'd downplayed his injuries to the medics. His face was mottled with bruises that had blossomed into deep purple patches. His lip and one eyebrow were split open while the other eye was nearly swollen shut. Dried blood caked his knuckles, and the left side of his ribs were marked with the same deep purple bruises that were on his face. He moved gingerly, obviously in a significant amount of pain.

"Roman. You need ice."

"Right now, I just need to be here with you." He held her a minute longer before tilting her chin up to him and examining her face. "I should have killed him."

"He'll suffer more this way."

"I'm going to make sure he does." He leaned down and kissed her lightly on her bruised lips before pulling her close to him again. They stayed in the embrace skin to skin until the water ran cold.

When they finally got out, she had him sit on the edge of the bed and used a first aid kit to rebandage the wounds on his face and knuckles before getting ice for his face, hand, and ribs. She looked him over as he lay there battered, because of her, ice packs obscuring his eyes. "Roman... Thank you."

He scooped her toward him and held her against his uninjured ribs, resting her head in the crook of his arm. Above them, the moon and stars looked down through the skylights. His voice rumbled in his chest. "Thank you, *mi cielo*. For coming back to me."

Epilogue

One year later

Shay ran a cloth over her worktable, sweeping up the last of the metal shavings left behind by her class. Today, she'd taught them how to make a simple pendant to hang on a chain. Everyone had finished in time to be wearing their creations when the shuttle arrived to take them back to the resort.

She walked to the back of the barn and leaned against the wide door frame. Both doors were propped open, letting in a cool breeze. Golden sunlight filtered through the forest as the sun dipped below the tree line, and Shay took a deep breath. The air was always sweeter here, so close to the stream.

When Roman had offered to find another location for her workshop or to tear down the barn and build something new, she'd refused. Instead, she insisted on being part of the work crew that gutted the inside. It was the place where she'd finally stopped running from Kyle. Every board they ripped up came with a sense of progress, but when she pried out the nails that he'd used to secure the chairs to the floor, she finally felt free.

The rest was all rebuilding. And what they rebuilt was even better than what had been there to begin with.

The sentencing hearing last month was hopefully the last time she'd ever set eyes on Kyle. Agent Hiller hadn't been bluffing about his dad being done with him. Without his help, Kyle found a lawyer willing to take the case pro bono, but there was no way of fighting the DNA evidence. The nail in his coffin was that he'd recorded the night in the barn with Shay and Roman through his webcam. Any doubt in the juror's eyes was gone by the time the brutal video ended.

He was convicted of three murders, including Valerie's, along with a laundry list of other charges from stalking to assault. After the judge ruled in favor of the maximum sentence, the guards started to lead Kyle, head down, from the courtroom.

Roman squeezed Shay's hand and raised his voice as they passed by. "Enjoy your cage."

Shay leaned into him, hugging his arm. Those were the exact words Kyle had said to him when he was detained at the police station, waiting for ICE.

Kyle's head shot up. Eyes wild, he lunged toward Roman. Limited by shackles, he didn't get close before the guards were on him. The sounds of his struggle threatened to follow them as Roman led the way out of the courtroom but faded away when the door swung shut at their backs.

Here, on the island, watching the sunset from the barn that had become a place of peace for her, that all felt like a lifetime ago.

A familiar rumble grew louder, and Shay smiled. With Gisella away on a month-long honeymoon, Roman had taken every opportunity to use the four-wheelers.

Shay closed the double doors and checked that the soldering irons had cooled down. Satisfied that everything was taken care of, she stepped out the front door into twilight, pulling it closed behind her.

At the edge of the woods, fireflies were flickering into existence, but her gaze was trained on Roman. Hands in his jean's pockets, he wore an untucked white T-shirt and leaned against the four-wheeler.

Shay's heart leapt, landing in an erratically happy pattern when she got close enough for her knees to brush his. With him still leaning against the four-wheeler, it gave her the unusual advantage of being slightly taller.

Crystal-blue eyes sparkled as they bore into hers, and he laced his fingers behind the small of her back. "What are you doing with the rest of your life?"

Shay's thumb rubbed the band that had been on her left ring finger since Roman had offered it to her the night after Gisella and Pete's wedding. He hadn't wanted to steal Gisella's spotlight by doing it before. And he had an elaborate proposal planned for next month—champagne, candlelight, a live violinist…but they'd gotten caught in a downpour walking home from the hotel and ran the rest of the way, laughing and only slowing down to kick rapidly forming puddles toward one another. When they got into the house, Shay was breathless and still laughing. Then, wringing water from her hair, she turned to find Roman on one knee.

His proposal was simple. "I can't wait anymore."

Even three weeks later the happiness in the memory still made her lightheaded, and she put her hands on his chest.

Roman cocked an eyebrow. "Still no answer for me?"

She slid her hands up to wrap around his neck and leaned in, letting her lips graze his. "I plan on spending the rest of my life with you."

A low growl rumbled in his throat, and he stood, scooping her into his arms to deepen their kiss.

He pulled back from the kiss, the lightness in his eyes replaced by something so intense it made Shay catch her breath. His brows knit together, and his voice cracked with emotion. "*Mi cielo,* you are my life."

A word about the author...

Josie Grey comes from a long line of story tellers. She's carrying on the tradition with her own blend of suspense and romance. When Josie isn't writing, she can be found practicing yoga or spending time with her two young sons.